Jewel Lagoon

Jewel Lagoon

Karen McMillan

Duckling
publishing

A catalogue record for this e-book is available from the
National Library of New Zealand.

ISBN: 978-0-473-42754-2

Designed by CVD Limited (www.cvdgraphics.nz)
Illustarions by Dmitry Chizhov

Printed by Choice Company, Taipei, Taiwan

For Milla McKenzie-Brown
with love

Contents

Chapter 1

A Day at the Beach has an Unexpected Ending

Ethan's plane looped tightly around the girls' heads.

Kiri turned to Emma, who was lying next to her on the beach. 'It's hard to believe that irritating wart is your brother. Leave us alone,' she yelled after him.

'I'm not doing anything,' shouted Ethan, fiddling with the knobs on the remote. The plane circled still closer to the two girls. 'You both talk too much. Blah, blah, blah. I wish you'd shut up.'

'We're talking about understanding dreams,' said Emma in a mild voice. She fingered the book in her hands and then squinted towards Ethan, brushing her long blonde hair out of her face. 'That's not a blah topic. It's useful information to know.'

Emma pulled at the hem of her light blue sundress, which was the same colour as her eyes. 'Listen to this, Kiri. Dreaming about flying means you have a feeling of freedom instead of being restricted and confined.'

'I suppose you had a dream about flying because it's the holidays and we don't have to be at school.' Kiri began towel-drying her dark, wavy hair, which was still wet from a day spent swimming and leaping through the waves like a dolphin.

'Strange though, don't you think? I really like school.'

'I know you do.' Kiri turned to look at her best friend and shrugged. 'You're crazy, you know. But come on, you've just spent the day lying around in the sun reading books – that's better than being stuck in maths class. Even you find maths boring.'

Ethan finally turned the plane out to sea. 'It's just a book and won't help you in the real world,' he muttered, squinting through his round glasses while the toy plane zoomed back and forth against the backdrop of a fiery sun. His face was creased in concentration when three pairs of hands unexpectedly grabbed him.

'Who said you could fly that plane on our beach, you redheaded freak?' said the ugliest and fattest of the three boys.

The fat boy grabbed Ethan by his checked shirt and hauled him to his feet. His second-in-command, a mean-looking boy with a shaved head, twisted Ethan's arm behind his back. The final of the thuggish trio, a boy with an unusually large nose, grabbed the remote and began examining the controls.

Ethan had encountered these brutes before and had always come out the loser, but still he struggled. 'Give that back to me!'

'Hey, leave him alone!'
shouted Kiri.

She jumped to her feet and ran towards the tussling boys. She glanced back to see Emma gazing in the direction of her parents, Mr and Mrs Lunny. They were lying further up the beach under an enormous orange sun umbrella, slathered in sunblock and fast asleep. They couldn't expect any help from them. Kiri gestured for Emma to follow, which Emma did nervously, clutching the book about dreams to her chest like a shield.

'Your girlfriend is coming to rescue you,' said the fat boy in a sing-song voice, shoving Ethan so hard that he almost lost his balance.

'Leave him alone!' Kiri ran up to the fat boy and slapped him on his arm. He ignored her and shoved Ethan again – this time so hard that Ethan tumbled to the ground.

'Your girlfriend has come to rescue you! Your girlfriend has come to rescue you! That's because you can't save yourself, you skinny toad!'

Kiri hit the fat boy on the arm again, but he continued to ignore her.

'She's not my girlfriend,' said Ethan, trying to get to his

feet, but this time the boy with the shaved head shoved him, knocking him back down. The boy with the big nose laughed manically while he nose-dived the toy plane into the sea.

'Stop it!' wailed Emma, inching close behind Kiri.

'Oh – and now your stupid sister is here too. Can't defend yourself, you freckled freak, can you? Loony Lunny! Loony Lunny!'

A boy they had never seen before swaggered over and stood squarely in front of the fat boy. He was taller and clearly the fitter of the two as he eyeballed the fat boy from beneath a tousled blond fringe.

'Leave him alone,' the mystery boy said in a low grumble.

'Who are you?'

'The name's Jed, and I don't like people like you.'

'People like who?'

'Snivelling, cowardly, low-life cretins who make trouble for other people when they should be minding their own business.'

The fat boy seemed unable to think of anything to say in reply, so for a moment the two boys simply glared at each other. The tension rose when the other two bullies moved closer to the fat boy, their eyes alert and rat-shiny, fists clenched ready for a fight. Ethan quietly got to his feet, picked up his blue backpack, slung it on to his shoulders and moved in behind Jed. It seemed like a stand-off. Suddenly, the fat boy went to punch Jed, but just in time Jed swung back out of reach, avoiding his fleshy fist.

'Run!' cried Kiri – and Jed, Emma and Ethan turned and followed her lead.

'Get them!' shouted the fat boy.

Kiri looked back to see him setting off with an ungainly stride, already panting because he was overweight and unfit. His second-in-command promptly tripped over a piece of driftwood, picked himself up and joined in the chase. The third of the trio spent a moment trying to stuff the remote for the toy plane into the pocket of his baggy shorts. When it wouldn't fit, he threw the remote down on the sand in annoyance and joined in the pursuit.

So all of them ran and ran until they had covered the length of the beach, ignored by the adults, who were busy with the books they were reading or the children they were nagging to pack up their wet togs and towels, picnic hampers and sporting equipment. Mr and Mrs Lunny continued to doze under their orange sun umbrella. At the end of the beach was a sheer cliff that stretched into the sky before dropping off abruptly. Kiri looked behind her – the three bullies were huffing and puffing up the beach but were not far behind their prey. The four children slowed to a fast walk, circling around, looking for an escape from the dead end they had come to.

Jed was the one who saw their escape path first, and Kiri blinked when she heard him gasp. There was a thin pathway of sand skirting around the bottom of the cliff. It could take them around the other side!

'Follow me,' Jed cried, leading them on to the small sandy path.

They turned the corner and Jed nearly ran straight into a palm tree. Inexplicably, there were a dozen or more palm trees in a cluster and the sand stretched smooth and wide as far as the eye could see.

'This wasn't here before,' said Emma in a small voice, breathing heavily, still clutching her book. 'We've been coming to this beach every summer for the past five years and this sand has never been here before – or these palm trees.'

'Must be man-made,' said Ethan, gasping for air.

For a moment Kiri thought this was a good explanation, until Emma said, 'But it wasn't here yesterday. I don't think anyone could make something that quickly.'

Kiri could hear the three bullies shouting at them from around the corner of the cliff. She would have continued running, wondering at the same time where this new piece of the coastline had come from, if the sand under their feet hadn't suddenly begun to ripple. It formed skinny ridges and appeared to be stretching. Around them the sand moved in towards the line of the cliff and far, far out in front of them. There was a loud pinging sound and then the children were catapulted backwards. Jed clung to a tree while the others were thrown into the air.

'Grab a tree!' he shouted, while the sand poured past his feet.

Kiri tumbled forward to land in the sand, but in five

quick steps clutched a palm tree to her like Velcro, spitting sand from her mouth. Ethan rolled backwards and, through accident rather than skill, found his own palm tree to cling to. Emma was flung back and was in danger of hitting her head on the base of one of the trees when there was another loud pinging sound and the sand suddenly shifted in an entirely different direction. She was thrown forward and then to the left, the book about dreams flying through the air from her grasp.

'Ahhhh!' Emma screamed
as she went flying past Jed.

'Grab my hand!' Jed shouted, throwing out his arm to her.

Emma grappled desperately. 'I can't,' she said, but at that same time their hands connected. Jed grimaced as he tried to hang on to the palm with one hand and keep hold of Emma with the other.

All of a sudden everything was still. For a moment there wasn't sound or movement, and tentatively the children let go of their trees. After seeing Kiri's raised eyebrows Emma became aware she was still holding Jed's hand. She let go of it abruptly, her pale face flushing the colour of tomato sauce. The four of them stared around in wonder. They were now standing on a small, almost perfectly round island. In the middle of level sand were sixteen palm trees in a symmetrical arrangement – four rows of four trees. Waves from the sea lapped the island gently, and far off in the distance was the beach that they had just run along. They could just make out the three thugs, who looked like little bugs jumping up and down on the sand. They could see the far-off orange dot that was Mr and Mrs Lunny's sun umbrella.

They stared at the scene before them and then they stared at each other.

'What just happened?' asked Kiri.

Chapter 2

Mr Jollybowler, Rinaldo the Parrot and the Decision of Where to go Next

There was silence while the four children pondered why they were standing on a tiny island, far out to sea, that hadn't been there moments earlier.

'I think we've just experienced a sideways earthquake,' said Ethan importantly, patting sand from his old-fashioned long trousers and shirt. Jed nodded enthusiastically, Emma's face wrinkled into a small frown, and Kiri choose to ignore his comment completely.

'Well, I guess we don't need to worry about those three boys now,' said Jed, slapping Ethan on the back in a friendly way.

'Thanks for coming to help,' said Ethan, sticking out his hand rather formally. 'I'm Ethan. I think I could have handled the situation–' Kiri snorted slightly, so Ethan raised his voice. 'But it's always nice to have some help.'

Jed shook Ethan's hand heartily. 'I'm Jed.'

'I don't think I've seen you around before,' said Ethan.

'That's because I only moved here recently.'

Kiri cleared her throat. 'I'm Kiri, and that's Emma. She's my best friend.'

'Emma's my sister,' said Ethan possessively. 'My twin sister.'

Emma ignored the introductions and instead gazed out to sea. Tears began to fill her blue eyes. 'How are we going to get back home? I can't swim that far.'

Kiri followed Emma's gaze with concern and put her arm around Emma's slim shoulders. She was about to say that it didn't look that far, but then remembered she was a strong swimmer and Emma didn't even like being in water. 'It's all right, Em. We'll think of something.'

Jed picked up Emma's book of dreams and handed it to her, avoiding her wet eyes. 'At least you still have your book,' he said kindly. Jed looked back towards the beach and then at the island. 'It does look too far to swim back, but I've just had a thought. We could chop down one of these trees and turn it into a canoe. Or chop a few down and make a raft.'

'Great idea,' said Kiri. 'But I'm not sure how we're going to chop down a tree. Does anyone happen to have a saw or an axe on them? Call me silly, but I forgot to pack them when I headed out this morning.'

'I've got a Swiss army knife,' said Jed, pulling a red-bladed implement from the pocket of his shorts.

'Excellent!' said Ethan. 'I've got some rope in my backpack.'

'Rope?' said Kiri.
'Who takes rope with them to the beach? You're weirder than I thought.'

'I needed rope for an experiment I was planning to conduct,' said Ethan defensively. 'Anyway, maybe we can lasso the top of one of the trees and pull it over. With our weight the trunk might break and then we can just hack through the rest with Jed's knife.' He looked at Jed for a moment. 'You look really fit and strong. This could work!'

'I enjoy playing sport,' Jed admitted. 'I'm looking forward to joining a new team after the holiday.'

Ethan bent down and began rummaging through his backpack. The oddest assortment of junk began to appear on the sand by his feet while he looked for the rope. Soon there was a pile of items that included an old television remote, several computer cables, batteries and a bicycle bell.

'Is that an old alarm clock?' said Kiri. 'Why would you want to bring that to the beach? I doubt it even works – it looks ancient.'

She picked it up and began to press some of the buttons.

'Don't do that!' Ethan shouted with alarm. 'Yes, it's an old clock, but I've modified it. Whatever you do, don't press the two red buttons at the same time.'

'Why not?'

'Because then the clock will blow up!'

'What?' Kiri set down the clock hastily. 'Have you completely lost your mind? What a knucklehead!'

'Don't worry – it's only a mini bomb. It's pretty harmless, really. Its main purpose is still to be an alarm clock, although it also doubles as a radio.' He took it off her and fiddled with one of the knobs. The sound of static filled the air. 'Blast, we must be too far out to sea, but the time is still accurate. 5.12 pm.'

'Is this a water pistol, mate?' said Jed, pointing at a plastic gun resting at the top of Ethan's pile.

'Sort of,' said Ethan, 'but I've changed it a bit. It still shoots water, but it also has a laser so you can shoot more accurately. Oh, and it has a siren.'

Jed nodded, looking impressed. 'What else have you got there?'

'Oh, never mind Ethan and his pile of junk!' said Kiri. 'He's always playing around with the most ridiculous things. What a dufus! We could be ages getting off this island and we have more important things to discuss. Like, for instance, does anyone have any food? I'm starving.'

Ethan rummaged further in his bag and held up a peanut butter sandwich that looked like it had been sat on.

Kiri made a face at the squashed offering. 'No one will want to eat that!'

'I will,' said Ethan, but Kiri noted that after taking another look at the sandwich, he quietly put it back in his backpack when he thought no one was looking.

'Sorry, but I haven't got anything,' said Jed, and he flushed slightly when his stomach gave a loud howl of protest.

'I've got chocolate,' said Emma, tearing her gaze from the far-off beach of home. She pulled a bar from the pocket of her sundress. 'It's not much, but how about I break it into four pieces and we can share?'

Everyone liked her suggestion, so Emma broke up the chocolate, making very sure that every piece was exactly the same size, and handed it around. They returned to the problem of cutting down a tree.

'We could use the alarm clock bomb to blow up a tree,' said Jed.

'YOU WILL DO NO SUCH THING!'

A loud voice came from behind them and the children turned in unison to see an enormous man walk out of one of the palm trees as though stepping through a door. When he turned and closed the palm door behind him carefully it was apparent he really had come through a door. The children stared at him, their mouths and eyes wide. He was wearing a floral skirt and he had a large bowler top hat on his head. A brightly coloured parrot of green, red and blue perched on his shoulder.

The man turned to face them, and contrary to his loud voice he had a beaming smile on his face. 'Ah, dear children! Sorry to have shouted, but we really can't have you blowing up anything on the island. Rule 44 says that no blowing up is allowed, unless you have permission from the Emperor of Highbottom – and that's not likely because he died fifty years ago. Poor chap. Such a shame.'

'Show us your biglietto! Show us your biglietto!' cried the parrot, peering at each of them in turn with his small beady eyes.

'Now, now, Rinaldo – don't be rude. We can get to the tickets all in good time.'

'Something tells me they don't have any biglietti,' the parrot said in a snide voice. He turned his head away from them and began humming a melody that sounded like Italian opera.

'Never mind him,' said the big man. 'He's always a bit grumpy before dinner. My name is Mr Jollybowler and I would like to welcome you to Elastic Island. Is this your first time with us?'

'Yes, it is, um, sir,' said Jed.

'Oh, right then. We'd better run through the safety procedures. It's all very basic. Make sure you hold on to a tree when the island is moving. Don't let go to scratch yourself or anything like that, or you'll get into trouble. Oh, and try not to sneeze, you could very well end up with sand up your nose. Not good at all. You can stow any luggage in the tree closest to you, but all luggage has to weigh less than twenty standard gold bars, and it needs to be physically no bigger than a small dog, although I'm sorry to say that dogs themselves are not allowed. We had a very pesky time with a pooch a few years back, so we had to ban them, you see. Any luggage over the prescribed limits will be thrown overboard – but don't worry, if you're lucky it will probably be here when we get back. That's assuming that it floats, of course. If it sinks you can say goodbye to it now.'

'Excuse me, Mr Jollybowler,' said Emma in a timid voice.

'But what exactly is Elastic Island? I mean, how did we get here?'

'Oh, I see now we shouldn't have started with the safety procedures. Elastic Island is the latest form of luxury transportation to all the islands in the South Pacific. I see you boarded from Browns Bay.'

'Luxury?' muttered Kiri, looking around at the tiny island of sand and trees.

'Palm trees, my dear,' said Mr Jollybowler. 'Our first model didn't have any palm trees, so there wasn't anything to hang on to when the island got moving. A bit of a flaw, we soon discovered, because everyone ended up in the sea. It's all right though. Only one person drowned. A rather nasty little man who was carrying a gun and had the audacity to point it at me. So between you and me, I'm not really that sad that he ended up on the ocean floor. It was a freak wave that did him in. I suppose I could have pulled him out, but I didn't really feel like it after the gun incident. Now, before we get underway, would you like a complimentary drink from the bar? Today we have a selection of raspberry and cucumber tea, banana and rhubarb cream and, finally, a Marmite shake.'

Mr Jollybowler had been talking so quickly that when he suddenly stopped, the children took a moment to realise that they had been asked a question.

'Stupido children,' muttered the parrot, before returning to humming Italian opera.

'I'll have a banana and rhubarb cream,' said Emma, and the others then made their selection.

Mr Jollybowler twirled on the spot, the parrot squawked 'bellissimo' three times, and suddenly there were four tall glasses brimming with brightly coloured drinks and decorated with little cocktail umbrellas and cherries resting in Mr Jollybowler's enormous hands. The children took them nervously.

'Oh, this is delicious!' said Emma, with evident surprise, after her first sip.

'Yum!' said Ethan, taking a second gulp of his Marmite shake.

'Wonderful,' agreed Kiri, for once having chosen the same type of drink as her best friend's annoying brother.

'Thank you, sir,' said Jed, gulping his drink of raspberry

and cucumber tea. He turned to Kiri and made a face that Mr Jollybowler couldn't see. 'This is gross,' he whispered. 'I don't suppose you want to swap?'

'Now where do you want to go? We have three destinations on offer today. Let me see.' Mr Jollybowler brandished a large, colourful printed brochure that included photographs and lines and lines of small print with times, dates and different destinations.

'Is Fiji on the list?' said Kiri. 'Or what about Tahiti? Or Vanuatu?'

'No, sorry, dear. They're not on the list for today. You can go to Gold Coin Port on Treasure Island, Stinky Fish Reef on Big Whale Island or Jewel Lagoon on Trinity Island.'

'But none of those are real!' said Ethan. 'Treasure Island is just a book. It's made up.'

Mr Jollybowler looked shocked. 'Of course it's real!'

Ethan wrinkled his nose in disbelief, but said anyway, 'If I had to choose – and these places were real – then I'd say let's go to Stinky Fish Reef!'

'I agree, let's go to Stinky Fish Reef!' said Jed.

'Hang on a moment! There are four of us and we all should have a say,' said Kiri. 'I want to go to either Treasure Island or Jewel Lagoon. I definitely don't want to go to anywhere involving stinky fish.'

'What a girl!' grumbled Ethan. 'Where do you want to go, Emma?'

'Um. I'm not sure,' said Emma. 'Mr Jollybowler, how do

we get back from these places? I mean, will we be able to get back home easily? Perhaps we should even go home right now.'

Mr Jollybowler turned over the brochure and began examining the return schedule. 'There is a return ride back to Browns Bay from Treasure Island on the twentieth of each month. You can get a ride back from Stinky Fish Reef once every six months. And there is a service scheduled at 5 pm every day from Jewel Lagoon for the rest of the month – with the time difference, that would give you a few hours to explore. I'm sorry; we can't just turn back right now, little miss, that would be in violation of rule 75. Once you have boarded Elastic Island you are committed to an outgoing destination. Clause 75 (f) allows some leeway in case of an emergency, but there is clearly no emergency today. The sun is shining, and you all look healthy and well – except perhaps for you, little miss, you could do with some building up, but that is going to take some time, so we need to continue.'

'Well, if we can't go straight home than I think we should go to Jewel Lagoon,' said Emma quietly, and everyone else murmured their agreement, although Ethan looked a bit grumpy they were missing out on visiting Stinky Fish Reef.

'Give us your biglietto! Your biglietto!' cried Rinaldo the parrot.

'Yes children, time to see your tickets,' said Mr Jollybowler, pulling out a chunky ticket clipper from his grass skirt.

'Um. We don't have any tickets.'

'Told you!' shouted Rinaldo. 'No biglietto, no ride-o!'

'Do behave, Rinaldo! I'm sorry, children, but we've only just started our service from Browns Bay, so I don't think everyone knows about the procedures yet. Have you seen any of our posters? Been to our ticket booth? Heard our advertising on late-night radio? No? Oh dear, well, payment for a ticket is quite simple really. Someone will need to sing us a song. Well, preferably all of you, but in this case I realise you won't have prepared anything, so one person will do.'

'Today we would like to hear Italian opera!' cried the parrot, beaming with a huge smile. 'Follow me.'

'I don't know any opera songs,' said Kiri.

'I can't sing,'
said Jed and Ethan almost in unison.

Emma said nothing. She simply bit her lip.

'Hush, Rinaldo. They don't need to sing an Italian song. Why would they do that? They're not Italian!'

'Would a Māori song be okay?' said Kiri suddenly. 'I don't mind being the one who sings.'

Emma smiled and the boys looked at Kiri gratefully.

'Of course, my dear,' said Mr Jollybowler.

Kiri began singing in a warm, clear voice, her song lifting gently into the early evening air.

Pōkarekare ana
ngā wai o Waiapu
Whiti atu koe hine
marino ana e
E hine e
hoki mai ra
Ka mate ahau
i te aroha e

When she had finished, for a moment, there was complete silence – and then Rinaldo the parrot burst into uncontrollable sobbing. 'Bellissimo! … That was so beautiful o! … Oh … Mamma Mia, an angel is standing amongst us-o! Pōkarekare ana-o … Pōkarekare ana-o!'

Kiri looked around at the others bashfully. Jed gave her a thumbs-up sign.

'That was great,' whispered Emma. For once Ethan grunted in agreement.

Mr Jollybowler pulled a white linen handkerchief from the waistband of his grass skirt and delicately wiped away a tear that had formed in his eye. 'My dear, that was wonderful,' he said. 'Simply wonderful!'

He put the handkerchief away and handed each of the children a small orange ticket, clipping the tickets as he did so.

'And for you, my dear,' he said to Kiri, 'here is the Elastic Island schedule. We look forward to hearing your wonderful singing again in the future.'

Kiri took the paper, carefully folded it and put it in her shorts pocket.

'Hold on to a palm tree, children!'

Already the sand was flying past their feet, the island stretching towards the horizon.

'Next stop Jewel Lagoooooooooon!'

Chapter 3

An Encounter with Chief Namba and his Apes

After saying their farewells to Mr Jollybowler and Rinaldo the parrot (who was still sobbing quietly to himself and muttering in Italian and broken English about the beauty of Kiri's song), the children set out to explore Jewel Lagoon. A sense of adventure seized them, although the girls were nervous when Ethan reset his alarm clock. They hoped he wouldn't blow them up.

'That's better,' said Ethan with satisfaction. 'All set for 1.55 pm with the change in time zone.' He put the alarm clock away in his backpack and then noticed Kiri's and Emma's worried gazes. 'Um, do you want a peanut butter sandwich?' he asked Emma, perhaps thinking food would take away her frown.

'No thanks,' said Emma, but she gave him a smile.

Jed and Kiri led the way forward. 'Wow, look at this beach,' said Kiri. 'It's so beautiful!'

White sand like they had only seen before in travel brochures stretched as far as the eye could see both left and right, the beach framed by thick native bush with plants that grew lush and green, swaying in the warm breeze.

The waves gently rolled back and forth against the sandy shore.

'Look at this!' said Jed.
'These look like jewels of some sort.'

In the sand glittered numerous objects that were bright like diamonds, but on closer inspection were round stones.

'Let me see,' Kiri said.

Jed picked some jewels out of the sand and held them up. In his hand were five round, shiny stones. They were brilliantly white, but there were flashes of blue and green and yellow and brown depending on which way he positioned them in the sunlight.

'I've never seen anything like them before,' said Kiri. 'They look like big white pebbles, but they are so sparkly – and look at all those different colours.' She noticed something else in the sand and bent to retrieve two shells. She studied them closely. 'What amazing shells! They look so symmetrical and the colours are beautiful.'

'Can I see?' asked Emma as the twins caught up with the rest of the group.

'Sure!'

Both Kiri and Jed handed their finds to her. Emma and Ethan peered at the stones and shells closely. Kiri and Jed walked further up the beach away from the sea. A movement in the dense bush caught their eye.

'I think it might be an animal or something,' Jed said to Kiri as she followed his gaze and they stepped nearer to the tropical bush.

Suddenly, wild cries filled the air, and a dozen dark, hairy figures stormed on to the beach, screaming and shouting. Jed instinctively rolled for cover behind a log, and a split second later Kiri made the same move. For a moment all they could hear were feral cries and the sound of Emma screaming. Jed lifted himself up and peered over the log.

'What is it?' whispered Kiri.

'Um … small monkeys,' whispered Jed, lowering himself back down again.

He held his finger to his lips and gestured for her to keep quiet. Unable to contain her curiosity, Kiri edged up to look over the log. She came back down in a hurry. The hairiest, meanest-looking apes she had ever seen were dancing in circles around Emma and Ethan, who were being held by two of the biggest apes.

'Small monkeys? They look like giant apes!' she hissed. 'They'll tear Emma and Ethan apart!'

The terrible sounds began to subside and Jed rose to have another look.

'They're taking them away,' he whispered. 'We should follow at a distance and when the time is right we'll come up with a plan and rescue them. My old coach always said it's good to work out a plan before play.'

'No! We need to do something now. Emma will be terrified,' said Kiri, and before Jed could argue with her she leapt from their safe hiding place and charged towards the apes, screaming at the top of her lungs. Jed shrugged and then followed.

'Wait for me!' Jed cried.

They tackled two of the closest apes, and for a moment their surprise attack was successful and the apes tumbled to the ground. But they were quickly surrounded by the rest of the apes and subdued. Hoisted on to the back of an ape, Kiri could only see the others awkwardly from her upside-down position. She watched while they were also heaved on to the backs of other apes. One of the beasts ripped the dream book from Emma's hands and sniffed it, causing Emma's eyes to grow even wider with fright. Ethan was desperately trying to hang on to his backpack. Jed fought valiantly against the ape who was trying to lift him before conceding defeat. To Kiri's disgust the apes were not just big, but they also smelt very bad. In hindsight, Jed's idea of having a plan would have been better.

Kiri had no idea how long the apes ran through the bush. She shut her eyes many times to avoid looking at their faces when they came up close to her, baring their teeth. The apes ran on and on until the bush ended, and the children found themselves being carried along a broad road leading up a steep hill. All Kiri could see for miles and miles was jagged, square rock. There was now no vegetation. The landscape looked dead.

'Look,' mouthed Jed, catching Kiri's eye. He motioned his eyes up, and Kiri followed his stare. At the top of the hill, past the mammoth rocks, was a huge castle with intricately carved stone walls, large gates and pointed towers stretching up into the darkening sky. Kiri had never seen a building more elaborate, or more intimidating.

The apes powered up the hill with the children on their backs, continuing to jabber amongst themselves. It was only when they neared the imposing gate of this enormous building that they fell into a subdued silence. Apes poised on the battlements shouted the order for the huge gates to be slowly swung open, after which they went through into a large courtyard, the walls adorned by carvings of warrior apes and men. The gates thudded to a close behind them and the apes swung the children off their backs to the ground. The ape that had been carrying Emma flung her book to the ground at her feet. She retrieved it and hugged it to her chest. Ethan protectively edged closer to his sister. Jed adopted a sporting stance, ready to take action when needed.

Horns sounded, and the apes bowed deep to the ground. A tall, imposing, dark-skinned man with long braided hair strode into the courtyard. A small monkey dressed in a straw hat and red waistcoat ran behind the man and screeched when he saw the children.

'Fall on your knees, you fools.'

A couple of the apes pushed them down and for a time all they could see was the elaborate bone sandals and the muscular legs of the man while he paced back and forth before them. There was another blast of horns and everyone rose to their feet, the apes pulling the children up. The children looked at the man nervously while he glared at them, his arms folded across his chest. He wore red cloth tied around his waist, in a style between a trouser and a skirt. His smooth dark chest was broad and adorned with a huge necklace of bone and ruby jewels.

'I am Chief Namba of Trinity Island,' he announced in a voice of immovable steel. 'Why are you children not in the mines? What were you doing on my beach? You'd better not have been trying to escape!'

The children glanced at each other, unsure what to say.

'SPEAK!' roared the Chief, focussing his bulging eyes on Ethan in a sudden movement that caused them all to jump.

'I don't know about any mines,' said Ethan in a high voice. 'We have travelled here from overseas.'

'Overseas? You mean you are not local children? You are not Trinitites?'

'I'm English, your Chiefness. So is my sister,' said Ethan, going red in the face.

'English? But England is a long way from here. What about you other two?'

'I'm American,' said Jed, his voice surprisingly firm.

'And you, girl, what are you?' said the Chief, turning towards Kiri.

For a moment she returned his stare and watched as his face began to crease with anger.

'I live in the Land of the Long White Cloud,' she said finally.

'We all live in the Land of the Long White Cloud,' said Ethan in a rush of words. 'People from all around the world live there.'

'The Land of the Long White Cloud?' The Chief suddenly looked alarmed. 'What is the purpose of your visit?'

'Please, your Chiefness. We are just here to … look at the scenery, that's all,' stuttered Ethan.

'I don't believe you!' roared the Chief, raising his fists in anger. 'You are here to spy on me. You are here to wage war!'

He suddenly noticed the stone jewels and shells that the apes had spilled on the ground before the twins. He bent down, gathering them in his massive hands, and let them rain through his fingers to the ground. 'And these! Did you gather these?'

'Ah, yes,' admitted Ethan.

'How dare you!' The Chief exploded with rage. 'Only my apes can gather these precious items. You have been stealing them – there is no doubt, look at your beady eyes and shiny ears. I order that you be executed tomorrow at dawn.'

At this news the little monkey at his feet clapped his hands enthusiastically. The apes seized the children and began dragging them towards a small door to the side of the main entrance. It was shaped like a carnivorous mouth. The children struggled, and Ethan's backpack and Emma's book tumbled to the ground.

'Wait!' roared the Chief. 'What's in that bag?' he asked, gesturing at Ethan's backpack. Then he noticed Emma's book lying on the ground next to it. 'And what is that?' he asked, picking up the book and leafing through the pages with his large hands.

'It's a dream book,' said Emma in a high-pitched squeak.

'What do you mean a dream book?' said the Chief in a harsh voice. 'Do you mean you read this and it makes you dream?'

'No, Chief Namba. It tells you the meaning of your dreams.'

'Really?' The Chief glanced at the book, stared at Emma with sudden interest and then handed her the book. His dark eyes took on a calculated look.

'I want you to interpret a dream for me,' he commanded. 'I dreamt last night that I was walking on the beach on a summer's day. The sky was very blue and I was flying a red flag. What does that mean?'

'Ah,' Emma fumbled through the pages. 'Well, Chief Namba, the fact that it is … summer, well, that … "foretells joyous events and prosperity". And the fact that you are flying a flag means … "you will have success in your undertakings". And the sky "signifies limitless freedom".'

The Chief grinned, displaying a pair of uneven, stained teeth. 'Well, is that so? Prosperity? Success in my undertakings and limitless freedom? Perhaps I shouldn't execute you after all.'

He stared at Emma for a moment, deep in thought, and she shrank from his unblinking gaze. 'I have decided you should stay as my guest. It seems you could be useful to me, that is, if you're not a spy or a member of any army.'

'I'm not a spy,' squeaked Emma. 'And I'm not in the army.'

The Chief looked her up and down, and then turned to look at Ethan. 'Perhaps you are right. Look at the pair of you, small, pale and pathetic. There is clearly nothing warrior-like about either of you.'

He turned to Kiri and Jed, who held his stare defiantly. 'Although the two of you look fresh-faced and more athletic. Perhaps you are young soldiers, or are here to spy on me!'

When they continued to stare at him in silence the Chief turned towards Emma. 'Prepare a room for the yellow-haired girl to stay as our guest. And arrange for some clothes she can wear to our feast tonight. We must show her the best of our hospitality because she has a talent for interpreting dreams.'

He clapped his hands loudly in the air; the castle doors opened and two mid-sized monkeys came scampering out. They too were dressed in straw caps and red waistcoats, just like the little monkey at the Chief's feet.

'Oh, a guest!' said one of them in a high, excited voice. 'It's so long since we've had a guest!'

He smiled at Emma with a joyful grin. The other monkey pulled a tape measure and began measuring Emma for her new clothes.

'Just turn this way,' he said while he held the tape measure this way and that. The two mid-sized monkeys began leading Emma into the castle.

'She's very pale, isn't she?'

'I think she'll suit lilac or a sparkly blue.'

'Oh, what a splendid idea! And how about a fine gold necklace to go with her dress? And what do you think about braiding her hair in the traditional style?'

'Excuse me,' interrupted Emma, turning to look back at the Chief. 'Ah … thank you for taking me in as a guest, but what about my brother? He's my twin brother, you know. And the other two here are my friends.'

Emma gazed beseechingly at the Chief while Kiri and Jed struggled with the apes that held them. A large ape held Ethan also, but instead of struggling Ethan appeared to be lost in thought. The Chief seemed about to order the children to be taken away when he glanced again at the bag on the ground.

'Boy,' said the Chief, suddenly staring at Ethan. 'What's in this bag? Show me.'

The apes released Ethan so suddenly he sprawled to the ground. He picked himself up and proceeded to rummage in his bag. Emma looked like she was about to cry. Finally, Ethan pulled out a long cylinder and handed it to the Chief. Kiri recognised it as an old kaleidoscope, and wondered, not for the first time, at the odd collection of junk Ethan had in his backpack.

'If you look through this end you'll see new universes,' Ethan announced in an extra-plummy British accent, and Kiri winced at the lie.

The Chief peered through the device and let out a grunt of pleasure.
'What is this, boy?'

'A universe far, far away,' said Ethan. 'And if you rotate the cylinder, you will see another.'

The Chief did as instructed and laughed out loud. 'This is wonderful, boy! All these universes at my fingertips, it is amazing.' He turned and addressed the apes. 'I have decided to let the red-haired boy live also. He is welcome at my palace as a guest. Let us bring him inside with his sister, and get him clothes suitable for our feast tonight. Let us eat chicken, roast pork and fried kūmara, coconuts, pineapples and bananas to celebrate having guests from the Land of the Long White Cloud!'

The mid-sized monkeys cheered and chattered together about fabrics and the cuts of various clothing, while the little monkey at the Chief's feet made a sulky face and crossed his arms in annoyance. The large apes lumbered off, while other mid-sized monkeys all dressed in straw hats and red waistcoats swept from the castle gates in a mood of celebration. Several of them retrieved the stone jewels and shells and took them inside. In the confusion, Ethan managed to hold on to his backpack, although several monkeys gestured that they wanted to carry it for him.

'But what about my friends?' asked Emma. 'Can they come too?'

The Chief turned to stare at Kiri and Jed for a moment before he made his decision.

'I still think you two are trouble,' he said. 'But for now you can join us for the feast.' He turned to one of the apes, who seemed to be in charge. 'Release the other children. They are from the Land of the Long White Cloud, so in hindsight, they may have information that is … useful to our cause.'

The apes released Kiri and Jed and they glanced at each other nervously.

'Welcome to my palace,' said the Chief as they stepped over the threshold of his home.

The little monkey who had been at his feet ran up his leg, climbed on to his shoulder and then leapt into the air. The creature attached himself to the elaborate chandelier that hung in the middle of the entrance foyer and peered down at them.

Kiri couldn't stop herself from looking around in wonder despite an ape that kept shoving her forward. Glittering jewels – diamonds, sapphires, emeralds and rubies – adorned elaborately carved furniture, mirrors and paintings. They proceeded through room after room, all decorated in this splendid manner. Kiri noted the way the light was refracted by the jewels. They gave out an eerie glow when you saw so many of them together – and all the mirrors served to exaggerate the effect. The rooms were decorated in the dark hues of blue, red or green.

The children were led to four separate, adjoining rooms. In each was a massive four-poster bed. The apes pushed each child into a room.

'I suggest you get ready for the feast,' said the Chief. 'My attendants will be along with new clothes for you soon, and then we will eat.'

Kiri had barely had a chance to look about the bedroom when there was a knock at the door and several monkeys entered the room. They fluffed and pulled and prodded, chattering excitedly the entire time – finally letting Kiri look at herself in the mirror. At first, she didn't recognise the girl in front of her. She wore a long emerald green dress that highlighted her dark skin, and the monkeys had piled her hair high on her head in a way that made her dark eyes look larger than they really were. She wore a gold necklace with brilliant emeralds. She didn't look like her usual tomboy self.

When she was escorted to dinner she did a double-take when she saw Ethan and Jed. Ethan had been transformed from the scruffy, redheaded boy in bad clothes to a young man dressed immaculately in a tuxedo. He looked so different Kiri found herself gaping at her best friend's brother, astonished at the transformation. Jed trailed behind Ethan looking handsome but uncomfortable in his tuxedo. He kept tugging at his shirt collar as though it were too tight. Then she saw Emma, completely transformed, and she gasped. Emma looked beautiful, her pale complexion perfectly complemented by a long, shimmering ice-blue evening gown. Around her neck was a delicate gold necklace with sapphire and diamond jewels. Kiri couldn't help but stare at how pretty Emma looked.

The four children were soon seated beside the Chief – the girls on one side, the boys on the other. A dozen mid-sized monkeys were also seated around a vast table that groaned under the weight of the mouth-watering food. The Chief had mentioned chicken and roast pork, but there were also turkey and ham, huge legs of lamb and plates of steaming sausages. Kiri could see trolleys waiting at the far end of the room laden with all sorts of exotic fruit, chocolate and ice cream and cake and mountains of different sweet treats.

'Now that our guests are here, let the feast begin,' announced the Chief.

Ethan and Jed tucked into their main course with gusto. Kiri and Emma exchanged a quick glance and it seemed the same thing was on their mind. Why was there so much food for so few guests? But eventually stomach rumbles caused Kiri and Emma to load up their own plates also. There wasn't much conversation for some time because everyone was too busy eating, the monkeys chewing noisily and making belching noises as they ate fruit from large platters.

After a third helping of dessert, Ethan and Jed finally pushed their plates away and the Chief stood up.

'To my guests from the Land of the Long White Cloud,' he toasted, holding a goblet of strawberry-flavoured foaming drink in his massive hands.

The children had been drinking the delicious liquid for the entire meal and it was making them feel very warm and contented in a strange, fuzzy way. All the monkeys jumped to their feet and toasted the children. Kiri glared at them suspiciously, while Jed just looked taken aback. Ethan basked in this sudden show of approval and smiled at them. Emma bit her lip.

A little later Emma managed a whisper. 'We have to get out of here, Kiri. I have a very bad feeling about all of this. We aren't guests, we're being held hostage! I want to go home.'

'It's night-time now and we've missed our ride home, so

we'll make a plan and go home tomorrow,' whispered Kiri before catching Jed and Ethan's eye. 'We leave tomorrow,' she mouthed.

Jed gave her the thumbs up, but for a moment Ethan pouted, seemingly taken by all the food and the attention. Only after Jed had elbowed him did he finally give the girls a reluctant nod.

After that the evening was strange and dreamlike. The Chief asked them numerous questions, but his voice seemed to come from a long distance away, and Kiri found that she had lost her voice while the room spun around them.

Chapter 4

An Interrogation

When Kiri woke the next morning, she couldn't quite remember where she was to begin with. The bed and pillow were wonderfully soft, so she lay perfectly still in the huge four-poster bed for a while, looking about her. The room glittered with jewels. There were jewels around the ornate mirror that was opposite. Jewels were imbedded in the woodwork of the dresser and side drawers. There was a heavily carved, dark wood wardrobe, and that too was encrusted with jewels. The sunlight was peeking through the windows and the room seemed awash with sparkle. It was like waking up in an enchanted palace, she decidedly dreamily, and then shook herself awake.

Was this an enchanted palace? Last night seemed like a

dream when she remembered the heavy food and strange foaming drink. Combined with this remarkably comfortable bed it made her senses dull. She felt so strange – her head hurt, and her stomach felt sore and heavy. She shook herself awake once again with an effort. They had to get out of here and get home! Anything could happen to them if they stayed. She rose out of bed and dressed clumsily in her t-shirt and shorts. She found it hard to move her arms and legs.

When she opened the door two monkeys bowed before her, wishing her a pleasant morning.

'I assume you would like to breakfast with the Chief,' said the first monkey politely.

'Especially since the others are already with him,' said the other darkly. 'You've slept much too late. He won't be pleased, I can say that much.'

The monkey attendants led the way, and after sweeping through vast hallways and past many rooms as opulent as the one she had slept in, Kiri was eventually seated for breakfast at a small table beside Emma, who was dressed in her finery from the previous night.

'Nice dress and necklace,' said Kiri dryly in a low voice.

'It's pretty,' whispered Emma defensively. Then she moaned. 'I don't feel very good. My head feels sore, and I feel like I'm moving in slow motion.'

'Me too,' said Kiri, looking slowly around the room.

The Chief was dressed in a sapphire blue trouser-skirt, and a dramatic sapphire and bone necklace. Kiri noticed that all the monkeys were now wearing blue waistcoats instead of red. The little monkey who had been at the Chief's feet the day before sat on the edge of the table nibbling on some peanuts that he clasped eagerly in his tiny hands.

'You are late. That is unacceptable,'
said the Chief in a booming voice,

pausing to glance at Kiri disdainfully before he shovelled an enormous spoonful of custard into his mouth. Some of it dribbled on to his chin.

'Morning,' said Ethan in Kiri's general direction.

He was dressed in the pants and shirt from last night. He was also wearing glasses that had window wipers on them. Astonished, Kiri watched them swing back and forth. He was busy devouring a huge plate of bacon and eggs, all smothered with tomato sauce, and he didn't bother once to look at Kiri.

'What's with Ethan's glasses?' muttered Kiri to Emma.

'Chief Namba demanded he show him something else from his backpack so he put his joke glasses on. Thankfully Chief Namba seems to like them. He looked so angry before that, I was really scared.'

Jed, dressed in his shorts and t-shirt, was busy eating also, but looked up to mouth a 'hello' to Kiri. He looked tired and anxious. Like the night before there was an enormous amount of food, although the table was much smaller. Aside from bacon and eggs, there were baskets of muffins of every description imaginable; there were sausages and ham and fritters and mushrooms, Danish pastries and toast and jam, and huge platters of tropical fruit. Her head heavy and her stomach churning, Kiri reached for a dry piece of toast, hoping it would make her feel better.

The Chief ignored the children until he had noisily finished his bowl of custard. Then he abruptly turned his attention to Emma, who shrank nervously from him.

'Yellow-haired girl, I had a vivid dream last night that a large panther was walking through the palace. Tell me what that means.'

'I'm very sorry, but I left my book in the room,' said Emma.

'You did what!' The Chief put his fist on the table so forcefully the whole table rattled. 'First the dark-haired girl is late, and now you refuse to interpret my dream–'

'I can if I get my book.'

'How dare you interrupt me! That is it! It is time to get the truth from you children. You answered none of my questions properly last night, even though I asked politely. I am done with being nice to you since you just throw my hospitality in my face.'

He stood and towered over them, and clapped his hands twice. At the sound, a couple of attending monkeys ran from the room, and then the children could hear creatures marching through the palace. Soon a file of big, angry apes crowded the room.

'Seize these children and bind them!' shouted the Chief.

Before they could say or do anything the apes descended on the four children and proceeded with strong thick rope to bind them to their chairs. Kiri was almost overcome by the sour, sweaty smell of the apes while they tied them. The smell was even worse than the day before. The Chief stormed from the room, and monkeys trailed after him carrying platters of food so that the table was soon empty. The dozen apes that were left stood with their arms folded and stared menacingly at the four children.

For a brief time, all was quiet. Kiri turned and looked at the others. All of them had their hands tied firmly behind each chair, with multiple loops of rope around their torso holding them tight. Only their legs were free, but when Kiri tried to move her chair it wouldn't budge. It was too heavy. Jed was struggling furiously, his muscles bulging at the effort, but he was making no headway either. Ethan looked back at Kiri with an attitude of annoyance, now only one window wiper on his glasses swinging back and forth.

Emma stared at Kiri helplessly. 'Now what do we do?' she said quietly.

Before Kiri had the chance to reply the Chief entered the room carrying a huge spear. The children watched in horror as he approached them, brandishing it above his head several times before pointing its deadly sharp point in the direction of each child in turn from across the table.

'I want answers out of you,' the Chief thundered. 'Speak and tell me all that I need to know and you will live. Fail me and I will execute you.' He turned to glare at the two girls. 'How many people live in the Land of the Long White Cloud?' he shouted.

'Um … a bit more than four million,' Emma squeaked.

'Quite a few, but not too formidable,' he muttered. 'How big is your army?' he demanded loudly.

'I don't–' started Emma.

'Fifty thousand people,' interrupted Jed, shrugging his shoulders under the ropes that bound him.

'What sort of weapons do they fight with? Do they have spears? Tomahawks? Knives?'

'Um … spears,' said Jed quickly. 'Just spears.'

'How fit are your people?
How hard do they train for war?'

'No training at all,' said Jed. 'They just give them spears and tell them to go and fight.'

'Excellent,' said the Chief. 'It seems there is nothing to worry about if your army invades. But what about the animals? Do they fight alongside the people?'

'No, they don't fight,' said Jed.

'Well, only with each other … sometimes,' added Ethan. 'But not in the army.'

'They aren't in the army! Why not? Have they said why they won't take up arms?' The Chief seemed outraged.

'But they don't talk,' said Ethan. 'We can hardly ask them that!'

As soon as the words were out of Ethan's mouth it was evident that he had made a big mistake.

The Chief's face went red and he began to splutter. 'Liar! You are all liars. Any fool knows that animals talk.'

'But the apes here don't talk,' said Emma in a small voice.

'Silence!' the Chief roared. 'Of course the apes talk, foolish girl. They just use a different language from the one we're speaking now. You are trying to confuse me! You must be spies, but I have caught you out with my questions. I don't even believe you come from the Land of the Long White Cloud. I think you must be working for the Other Side, for the terrible Makana. Admit it, Makana has sent you here to spy on me.'

Then his speech became so incoherent, none of the children could understand him. It seemed he was speaking in a strange foreign language. 'Weit Smol! Mi no likim ia! Mi wantem gowe! Mi harem trot …'

Kiri strained against the ropes that bound her, but it was no use. She racked her dull brain for a way out of their current predicament, but could think of nothing. She felt weighed down by the heaviness in her limbs. Minutes ticked by and the Chief finally seemed to calm down and began talking so they could understand him.

'You will be executed before midday' were his final, frightening words before he fell silent, his spear at his side like he had run out of energy. Suddenly Kiri's head cleared, she felt energised – and she had an idea.

'I know what your dream means,' said Kiri loudly, shattering the silence.

'I thought only the yellow-haired girl interpreted dreams!' The Chief held his spear towards her, his face dark and dangerous.

'We all do. But we each interpret them in different ways. She uses her special book, while the meanings of dreams come to me in visions,' bluffed Kiri.

'Well, girl, tell me.'

'NO.' Kiri's voice was firm.

'What!' The Chief inched the spear closer with an abrupt motion.

'You have to agree not to execute us. If you do, you'll never know what your dream means – and I can tell you that the meaning of this dream is very important.'

The Chief seemed about to begin another rant when the little monkey jumped on to his shoulder and whispered something into his ear. Kiri strained to hear and could just make out the words. The monkey seemed to be saying that the Chief should pretend to do what she had asked.

The Chief nodded, lowered his spear, and then said,

'Okay. I agree not to execute you.'

'Then release us from our bindings,' said Kiri.

The Chief narrowed his eyes at her.

'It would show you mean what you say,' she said. 'That you won't go back on your word.'

The Chief frowned, but then the little monkey whispered in his ear again and he ordered the apes to release them. While the apes were busy undoing their bindings, Kiri managed to catch the other children's eyes.

'We have to make a run for it,' she mouthed. She nodded towards the table. 'We should overturn that and then run.' The others nodded grimly, Emma's eyes wide and wet with tears.

When the bindings were off them, Kiri rose to her feet, rubbing her wrists where the ropes had dug into her skin. 'Chief, the meaning of your dream is …' She glanced at the Chief, who was paying close attention to her every word, and then she looked at the others and paused dramatically as she leant against the table, her fingers resting under its hard wood. Out of the corner of her eye she saw the others put their hands under the table also.

'RUN FOR IT!'

she screamed at the top of her lungs as together they sent the table flying towards the Chief and his apes. They streaked towards the door, making the most of the distraction, with Jed easily overtaking Kiri as they ran into the corridor.

'This way,' he shouted. 'Through this door.'

The children followed Jed into a large room, Kiri turning to see the apes charging behind them, their eyes burning with blood lust, and their mouths dribbling with the thrill of the chase. The children skidded through another door into a long corridor and then followed Jed into another room.

'Hurry!' said Kiri, turning to see Ethan and then Emma struggling to keep up behind them.

Then everything was a blur. Jed pulled Kiri into another side room, quickly shutting the door behind them. Through the cracks in the door they could see that the apes had captured Ethan and Emma, and soon after the Chief strode into the room. Kiri was about to cry out when Jed clamped his hand over her mouth.

'We can't help them if we are captured too,' he whispered.

He only removed his hand when she eventually nodded. They peered at their friends through the cracks of the door.

'Where are the other two?' screamed the Chief.

'I don't know, your Chiefness,' said Ethan, his voice trembling. 'We couldn't keep up with them. They must be far away by now. They went in that direction.'

Kiri sighed with relief when she saw him pointing past their door to another, larger room.

'Find the other children!' roared the Chief, and all of the apes, except the two holding Ethan and Emma, ran in the direction Ethan had indicated.

The Chief turned to the twins. 'You will be executed, and

when we find the other children they will be executed also.'

'That's not a good idea,' said Emma in a fast, high voice. 'You need us to interpret your dreams. Your dream of seeing a panther signals great danger to you, Chief Namba. I was scared to tell you before, but the panther symbolises a dark enemy that is soon to threaten you. But the fact the animal was walking through your palace also means that the dream will be the first of many that you will have about this enemy. Only if you understand your future dreams may you be able to defeat this enemy.'

The Chief stared at Emma for a moment and Kiri watched while her best friend tried to return his stare without blinking or showing fear. Finally, the Chief came to a decision. 'Then I will spare you, but execute your brother.'

'But he interprets some dreams that I can't. You need both of us.'

The Chief clenched his fists and muttered under his breath. Finally, in a low rumble, he said, 'Take these children to the mines. It seems they are useful to me, after all.'

'The mines?' said Ethan, shaking his head so abruptly that the remaining window-wiper on his glasses fell to the floor.

'It's either that or the dungeon, stupid boy,' spat the Chief. 'The mines mean you can stay alive … for a while. Or would you rather go to the dungeon?'

'Oh, no. The mines sound good,' said Ethan quickly.

'You had better be able to interpret any further dreams I have,' said the Chief fiercely.

He leant forward, his big hands threatening Emma's small neck, before ripping Emma's necklace from her throat.

'And that's mine, you little thief!'

he roared, leaving Emma looking flushed and startled. 'Take them away!' he thundered.

When he strode from the room there was the distinctive sound of metal hitting the palace floor. A minute later Kiri and Jed were peering through the door into an empty room. Both of them stared at a spot on the floor where a large key had fallen from the Chief's blue trouser-skirt.

Chapter 5

More Surprises Lie Behind Castle Walls

'Something tells me that key could be useful,' said Jed, peering into the empty room.

They opened the door they were standing behind as quietly as they could, looking around furtively. Kiri bent down to retrieve the large skeleton key. She turned it over in her hands before putting it in her shorts pocket.

'This key must open something important if the Chief was carrying it,' she said. 'It's definitely worth hanging on to, I'd say. But the big question is where are these mines that they are taking the twins to – and how are we going to get them out of there when we find it?'

'I guess we'll just have to go in the direction we saw them

leave,' said Jed. 'The apes make such a racket; we should be able to hear them from a mile away. At the very least we have to get out of this place – and then hope the mines aren't too far away.'

Jed stuck his head around the doorway and then gestured for Kiri to follow him. They stole down the marble corridor, alert for any sound. At the end of the corridor there were some stairs leading down. Jed looked at Kiri with raised eyebrows and Kiri nodded. Down they went into the gloomy stairwell. When they reached the lower level they discovered they were at the end of a long hallway with rough stone flooring – and this time with numerous closed doors on both sides. Above their heads was a huge metal security grate. Its long, pointed metal fingers looked deadly.

Kiri edged past Jed and tried the key from her pocket in the wooden door closest to them. It creaked open. Inside was a bare stone-walled cell, complete with a small barred window on the opposite wall.

'I think we've just found the dungeon,' she whispered.

'Let's open the next cell,' said Jed, peering into the empty cell from behind her. 'We might find something helpful.'

Kiri abruptly moved to the next door, opened it with the key and before Jed could catch up, she crossed inside.

'Oh, my,' she said.

There was an odd noise, like the wind gusting in waves. The cell was large enough to house twelve grown men, but instead it contained the huge form of a giantess, lying back against the wall, fast asleep and snoring through her wide-open mouth. She was wearing an enormous flowery sundress of pinks, reds and yellows. Acres of bright fabric moved up and down rhythmically with each snore. Curious, Kiri stood on tiptoe to look at her face. She had the biggest mouth Kiri had ever seen – and it was globbed up with bright red lipstick. Kiri edged away towards the door.

'Let's go before she wakes up.'

'Just what I was thinking,' said Jed.

Back in the hallway they relocked the door quietly and the noise of her snore instantly disappeared.

'That was a terrible sight!' said Jed.

'Actually, I thought she looked sad,' said Kiri.

'What? How can you tell? She was fast asleep and snoring.'

'But she was all dressed up with make-up on. It was like she thought she was going on a picnic on a summer's day, rather than sleeping in a yucky dungeon.'

Jed looked at Kiri liked she'd gone mad.

'Okay, then,' said Kiri, 'You choose the next door.' She handed him the key.

Jed selected a door four along on the right. He opened the door and quickly locked it again before Kiri could see inside.

'What was in there?'

'Lots of different creatures, all in chains, moaning and grinding their teeth. It wasn't very pleasant.'

Kiri stopped suddenly. 'You know, I think we need to be more sensible about this. There must be about forty cells here. If we're going to be checking out the dungeon properly then I think we will need to open every door and see what is inside.'

So that's what they did. They started at one end, opening cell after cell. Most cells were empty. Some had sleeping adults who refused to be woken. Two of the cells contained the oddest assortment of creatures they had ever seen. Then there was only one door remaining, the last door right at the end of the long hallway.

'Lucky last,'
said Kiri, opening the lock.

But this time it wasn't a dungeon cell; instead it was another hallway where rough stone gave way to elegant marble tiles.

'This must be another part of the palace,' Jed said when he walked through the doorway.

Kiri followed, taking the key, and leaving the door open and unlocked so they would know how to get back if they needed to.

Together they edged along the hallway until they came to an open courtyard. It had a huge, jewel-studded fountain in the middle that glowed in blues, reds and greens, with jewel-encrusted dark wooden seats scattered amongst the fernery. Sunlight filtered through the semi-open ceiling, and the courtyard sparkled and shone with dazzling colour.

'Wow,' said Kiri, momentarily distracted. 'This is beautiful.'

'This must have cost a fortune!' Jed exclaimed.

There were a number of rooms off the courtyard, so it was difficult to know which direction to go in. Kiri looked at Jed quizzically, but he just shrugged his shoulders.

'Okay, let's try here first,' she said, leading the way into the room opposite.

They walked quietly through rooms of opulent finery. It may have been Kiri's imagination, but the rooms seemed even more luxurious than the upper level of the palace. There were so many rooms, each of which could have housed a family.

'Where is everyone?' whispered Kiri.

'It's odd isn't it? All these rooms, all this furniture, but no people,' Jed whispered back.

They had only gone through a couple more rooms when they came upon a curious sight. Up until now every room had been decorated in red, green or blue, with jewels dripping from every surface, but now they entered a room that was empty. It had a marble floor and plain white walls. There wasn't a jewel in sight. It also had huge steel doors that took up an entire wall. The doors didn't have any handles.

Kiri reached out to touch one of the steel doors and was jolted by a shock of electricity. She fell to the floor, her hand burning painfully.

'Are you okay?' In his haste to see if she was all right, instinctively Jed bent down and clasped her close while he carefully examined her hand.

'I'm okay,' said Kiri as the burning began to ease.

They looked each other in the eye. Kiri noticed that Jed had the dreamiest green eyes, and then she felt her cheeks burn. Jed dropped her hand and abruptly walked towards the steel door. Kiri got to her feet and shook her hand slowly. It seemed all right.

'I wonder what's behind these doors,' Jed said.

'How do we get through them?' said Kiri.

They couldn't see a control panel, or any device that would open the door. Sensibly, Kiri didn't want to try touching the door again.

There was a sudden noise – the sound of an army marching through the palace. A steady thumping of feet shattered the previous silence. Grunting and wild screams filled the air.

'That must be the apes,' said Kiri.

'We have to get out of here!'
said Jed.

They fled in the direction they had just come. On they ran through corridors and rooms, finally emerging in the courtyard and then through the hallway that led to the dungeon – all the time the grunting and shouting of the warrior apes growing louder and louder.

The children raced down the marbled hallway just when a group of apes entered the courtyard. Kiri turned in terror as they charged towards her and Jed. The children made it through the door to the dungeon just as one of the apes tried to tackle Kiri. She slammed the door in his face and fumbled with the key in the lock.

'Hurry!' cried Jed, racing ahead.

Kiri followed Jed, slipping the key into her pocket. They could hear the apes on the other side ramming the door with a heavy object. The door began to shudder against its hinges. They sprinted up the dungeon hallway, watching in horror as the large metal grate with its deadly long spears began to grind slowly towards the floor. Jed slid under the grate, urging Kiri to follow, and the apes burst through the far end door. The apes swarmed into the dungeon corridor, howling and shrieking. Kiri could feel them gaining on her as the metal grate sank lower and lower.

'Come on!' shouted Jed, pausing to wait for her on the other side.

With only inches to spare, Kiri rolled under the metal grate, seconds before it crashed to the floor. Jed pulled Kiri to her feet and they raced up the staircase, Kiri turning to see the apes using their brute strength to slowly raise the grate.

They raced through the upstairs corridors and rooms. Kiri's lungs burned and her heart raced with the effort. She tried to fight down her panic. Jed wasn't even breaking a sweat.

'How do we get out of here?' she panted. 'Which way do we go?' She turned towards the room they had recently hid in.

'No!' said Jed, dragging her in the other direction. 'We

already know that's a dead end. Let's try this way.'

There was a massive roar from below them, and then they could hear the sound of apes thundering up the stairs.

'They've broken through,' said Kiri.

'Look, there's light under that door. Try the key, Kiri.'

Kiri looked in the direction Jed was pointing. There was a large wooden door, and her spirits lifted at the sight of sunlight streaming under the crack in the door. Kiri fumbled with the key in the lock.

'Hurry!' said Jed, looking behind them.

She finally managed to get the key to turn and together they flung the heavy door open. They looked out and saw that they were at the back of the castle and the door opened out on to the top of the steep, rocky hill. Kiri turned to see the apes charging towards them.

'Let's get out of here,' cried Jed, stumbling down the steep path.

Kiri stepped outside, straining to close the door behind her before locking it. She then skidded down the steep path behind Jed.

They finished their descent, Kiri bruised and breathless, as the apes began pouring through the main castle gates. The children set off at a frantic run, stumbling through the dense bush, the cries of the apes seeming to be only inches behind them.

Chapter 6

Pangali the Platypus Resolves to Help

Kiri and Jed fled through the bush until they could no longer hear the screams of the apes.

'Let's rest for a moment and think about what we're going to do next,' said Jed.

'Good idea,' said Kiri, panting.

The two searched for a place to sit and then collapsed gratefully by a small river. Kiri dangled her feet in the water, enjoying the cool sensation on her hot feet.

'Ouch!' said a small voice. 'Would you mind not doing that?'

Kiri lifted her feet out of the water quickly, and both she and Jed peered in the water to see who had spoken. They couldn't see anything out of the ordinary. It was a just a typical river with grassy banks that gave way to a muddy, stony riverbed. There was nothing to see except for stones and logs.

'Who's there?' asked Kiri.

Then what she thought was a small log suddenly moved and she realised it was not a log but a duck's bill. But then the rest of the creature's body came into view and she realised it was not a duck either. The creature was furry with four small webbed limbs and a long broad furry tail.

'It's a platypus!' said Jed,

and when Kiri looked at him questioningly, he shrugged. 'I've seen them before on a trip last year – although never a talking platypus!'

'I'm Pangali,' said the platypus in a slow, depressed voice, seeming not to have heard Jed's identification of his species.

The children introduced themselves, there was a moment's pause and then the platypus started to sob.

'What's the matter?' asked Kiri.

'You're the only creatures I've seen, apart from some birds, since I lost my family,' said Pangali.

'Oh, that's terrible!' said Kiri, her voice full of compassion. 'How did you lose your family?'

'Platypuses live on the other side of the island at Free Bay, and one day my wife and two children decided to go for a day trip, so we swam inland through to Black Mountain and had ourselves a little picnic.'

Kiri wanted to ask what was involved in a platypus picnic, but decided not to interrupt the mournful voice.

'There was a big rumble just as we were finishing our meal, and the ground heaved and rolled, and then a huge number of rocks poured into the river. Afterwards, I was stuck on one side of the rocks, and my wife and my dear children were on the other side. Thankfully, no one was hurt. We could shout to each other through the wall of rocks and my wife assured me that they were fine. We had tried for about half an hour to find a way through to no avail when there was another rumble and more rocks plunged into the river. I shouted for my family to swim home to safety and that is the last I have seen or heard of them in more than five years.'

Pangali's large brown eyes filled with tears and Kiri had to stifle a sob. It was one of the saddest stories she had ever heard. Kiri lived with her grandmother and she knew what it was like to have lost family members.

'The birds told me what had caused this to happen,' continued Pangali. 'It is because the evil Chief stole the Jewel Egg. When he and his apes lifted it from its resting place at the top of the Black Mountain, rocks began to crash down the mountain slope. Our lands have never been the same since thanks to his thieving actions.'

'Um, we've already had the misfortune to meet the Chief,' said Jed. 'But what's a Jewel Egg?'

'The Jewel Egg is a wondrous source of power and light – but now that power is in the hands of a madman. Chief Namba is the most terrible tyrant who ever lived!' cried Pangali, his small voice rising in outrage.

The air began to cool and the sun sank in the sky. The children had been running for hours. Kiri and Jed moved closer to Pangali to hear him better.

'He is the brother of the most famous royal figure of Trinity Island, the revered Princess Makana, who was in line to govern the entire island but now only rules over Free Bay. When Chief Namba stole the Jewel Egg, he stole much of the Princess's power and because of that he was able to seize Jewel Lagoon with his army of apes. And the Jewel Egg was also the only power source for Black Mountain, so since it's been stolen the centre of the island has been without light. It is a bleak and dangerous place now. It was a fearful time when Chief Namba announced war against his sister. The birds tell me of the terrible killings and torture that occurred.'

The platypus shivered. 'I won't speak more of that. It's too awful. The only good thing in this tragedy is my family are living in the peaceful place of Free Bay, far from the effects of war and all its suffering.'

While Pangali had been talking the light had almost faded, and Kiri looked about with sudden alarm. It was getting very dark.

She turned to Jed. 'We have to get going if we want to rescue Emma and Ethan. We need to find the mines.'

'The mines!' cried Pangali. 'But you can't go there. It's much too dangerous.'

'But we need to go there. The apes have captured our friends,' said Jed.

'This is dreadful! Dreadful! Your friends are doomed!' Pangali began to thrash about in the water in despair.

'Stop it!' shouted Kiri in a very loud voice. Pangali became still and stared at her with big moist eyes. 'Please calm down. We're going find the mines and we're going to rescue our friends, apes or no apes.'

Pangali sighed and was quiet for a moment. 'Let me help you then,' he said finally, in an even more depressed voice.

'Would you?' said Kiri, deliberately not commenting on the miserable tone of Pangali's voice. 'That would be so kind.'

'I know what it is to not be with a loved one,' said Pangali mournfully.

Kiri didn't count Ethan as a loved one, and of course, Jed barely knew either of the twins – but Emma was her best friend and was like a sister to her. She had to help her! 'Do you know where the mines are?'

'I have a good idea where the mines are, although I haven't been to them personally. The birds pass on information from time to time.'

'So shall we set off now?' she said. 'What's the best way to the mines?'

'The most direct route is to journey towards Black Mountain. You just follow the river and turn off on to a pathway further up and then follow that until you come to the mineshaft. Apparently, you can't miss it,' said Pangali.

'Sounds easy!' said Jed.

'But at night-time the ape patrols double their watch, the birds tell me, so you are sure to be caught. So even if you did manage to get to the mines, you wouldn't be able to get in. But you wouldn't want to go into the mines in any case, because no one ever comes out alive.'

Jed and Kiri stared at each other through the gloom, both of them wearing expressions of despair.

'But if we go in daylight you might have a chance of success,' said Pangali, just when it seemed all hope had gone.

'I've been told the apes often stop to eat, and sometimes to sleep, so we may be able to get you in and your friends out again without their noticing. Not that I've ever heard of anyone doing anything like that, but yes, I think as a plan it should work.' He sounded almost happy when he came to this conclusion.

'Yes, that should work,' said Jed, pleased they had a plan of action.

Kiri nodded. 'So we'll make a start in the morning?'

'We'll head off at sunrise,' said the platypus. Then he noticed that Kiri had begun to shiver with the cold. 'Come on, let's find you a place to rest, and I'll see if I can arrange some dinner for you. Follow me!'

Pangali plunged into the river, surfaced and began swimming ably upstream. Kiri and Jed followed along the riverbank, stumbling now and then over stones and bits of logs and all manner of other things that they couldn't see very well now the light had almost gone. Just when the children thought they could go no further, Pangali gave a shout and waved one of his webbed front limbs towards a small, secluded cave, not far from the water.

'Go in and make yourselves comfy. I'll go and find some food,' he shouted, and with a splash he was gone.

Jed took the lead and inched into the cave. 'I can't see, it's too dark,' he complained.

'I think we should make a fire.'

'How are we going to do that?' said Kiri. 'I know there are plenty of sticks and logs to burn, but how do we get it started?'

'Well, we could do it the old-fashioned way with two sticks, but that can take time.' Jed rummaged in his pocket and pulled out his Swiss army knife. 'This just happens to have a lighter on it.' He flicked it so a small flame appeared.

'Awesome!' said Kiri.

They quickly gathered wood and in no time Jed had a small fire blazing. They ventured into the cave and saw that it was full of twigs. It was dry but quite small. It would only just sleep the two of them, so it would be very cosy, cramped accommodation for the night. They looked at each other.

'Ah, I think I'll sleep out by the fire, if that's okay with you,' said Jed.

'Okay,' said Kiri, a little too quickly.

There was a shout from the river and Pangali appeared with a bulk of something in his bill, which he spat on to the grassy verge. 'Dinner's served!' he said.

Kiri and Jed walked to the edge of the river. At their feet was a wriggly, squirming selection of different creatures. Although she hadn't eaten since breakfast and she was very hungry, Kiri's stomach churned. There were worms and shrimps, water bugs, beetles and a small frog.

'Thank you for catching all of this,' said Jed slowly, 'but this isn't the sort of food that we eat.'

'Oh.' Pangali looked crestfallen. 'What do you eat?'

'Meat, vegetables, fruit – that kind of thing,' said Jed.

'Chocolate,' said Kiri.

'I'm sorry, but I can't offer you any of those things. And I don't even know what chocolate is!' Pangali's eyes began to leak tears. 'My first real guests in five years and I can't feed you. This is terrible!'

Jed bent down for a close look at the wriggly pile and plucked out a small shrimp. 'Wait a moment, this looks like something we can eat,' and he put it in his mouth, crunched on it and swallowed. 'That was delicious!' he said with a big smile.

'Really?' whispered Kiri.

'No,' Jed whispered back. 'But I bet it's better than a beetle.'

Pangali smiled and turned expectantly to Kiri.

'Oh, brother!' she said under her breath. She looked through the pile and selected another small shrimp and threw it in her mouth and swallowed it whole. 'Yes, delicious,' she managed, although the slimy sensation of it going down her throat made her want to throw up.

'Oh good!' cried Pangali. 'Would you like more?'

'I'm full now, thank you.'

'One was enough for me!'

Pangali smiled as though they had eaten a large feast and began gobbling the pile of wriggling creatures with joyful abandon. 'That's a good fire,' he said, with his mouth full. 'It gets very dark and cold now that the Jewel Egg isn't in its rightful place.' Indeed, it was now almost pitch black beyond the perimeter of the fire.

The children began to yawn while they watched the platypus finish his meal. It had been a long day. Jed's stomach rumbled, but he coughed to disguise the sound. Pangali noticed their yawns and urged them to go to bed. They were just about to head off when there was a mighty roar from far away and high up. It was a wailing, agonising bellow that went on and on and on.

'What was that?' said Kiri when it had finished.

'That is Olaf the Giant, the meanest giant that ever lived,' said Pangali. 'He lives high up on Black Mountain. He is evil, almost as bad as the Chief. Whatever you do, don't go near him – there is no telling what he might do. I hear that he is very violent.'

'Oh!' gasped Kiri.

'Why does he roar like that?' said Jed.

'I don't know,' admitted Pangali. 'But he roars like that every night, sometimes for an hour or more. I expect it is something dastardly.' He suddenly noticed the children's wide eyes, luminous in the dark. 'But don't worry dear children, he never comes down the mountain and we are many miles away. You are quite safe. Well, accept for the Chief's apes, that is.'

Pangali bid them good night and promised he would see them when the sun was up in the morning. The children sat by the fire for a time after Pangali had left, whispering in small voices, talking about anything and everything except what was really worrying them.

'So how did you meet Emma and Ethan?' asked Jed.

'I know Emma from school. We're in the same class and I was the person who was assigned to look after her when she first arrived from England.'

Kiri peered into the fire, remembering the little blonde girl who was so nervous and shy of everyone on that first day five years ago. Kiri had instinctively liked Emma and had made a point of looking out for her beyond that first day, when her duties were officially over. Then when Kiri's life was turned upside down several months later when her parents died in a car accident, Emma had been the one looking after her. They had been inseparable ever since.

'Ethan's her twin brother, so he hangs around when we're together – unfortunately.'

'They seem nice,' ventured Jed.

'Emma's the best,' said Kiri. 'But Ethan's a dork.'

Jed laughed. 'He seems like a good bloke to me.'

'Oh, let's not talk about Ethan. What about you? You said you were from America? If you don't mind me saying, you have a strange twang, a slightly weird way of talking.'

'And I thought my accent was changing. When I talk to friends in America now they say I sound different! But I've only been living in Browns Bay on and off for a couple of years, and only permanently since last week, so who knows what I'll sound like in the future.'

'Do you like Browns Bay?'

'Yes, I do. And I think I'll probably like it even more when we get home from here.'

'I sure wish we were home right now,' Kiri said.

After that they found they had run out of conversation and they decided they should sleep. But their unvoiced fears of roaring giants, screaming apes and their empty stomachs conspired against them, so it was no surprise that neither Kiri nor Jed slept much that night.

Chapter 7

The Journey towards Black Mountain

When Kiri woke with the first shards of daylight, she groaned as stiffness and cramp laid siege to her body. She slowly sat up, pulling twigs and sticks out of her hair. Her denim shorts and red top were filthy. Out through the entrance of the cave she could hear Jed moving around. She clambered painfully to her feet and hobbled out to see him. He looked as dirty as she was.

The fire was now out, but the sun was shining brightly in the sky, spreading welcome warmth through the limbs of the two children.

Jed's stomach grumbled. 'I'm so hungry; I think I could eat a feast of beetles and frogs now if I was offered.'

Kiri wrinkled her nose in distaste. 'Even if I was dying of hunger, I'd refuse.'

'No, you wouldn't,' said Jed. 'You like Pangali too much. I can tell. Speaking of which, let's find him so we can get moving.'

They walked along the edge of the river for what seemed like hours, but was really only minutes, calling Pangali's name.

'Oh, don't say he's abandoned us,' said Kiri.

She sat down on the ground with a thud and rested her head in her hands.

'I'm sure he wouldn't do that,' said Jed firmly. 'He seemed very reliable and very helpful – well, once he'd stopped being negative about everything. Besides, we are his first company in a long while. He'll turn up.' As Jed said this, out popped a familiar bill and then Pangali's furry body.

'Good morning, children,' Pangali said in a slow voice, rubbing his eyes with his front webbed limbs.

'Good morning,' said Jed.

'Where did you come from?' said Kiri.

'Just from one of my burrows. Quite a nice one, even if I say so myself.'

Kiri leaned over the edge of the riverbank and saw that beneath some overhanging vegetation she could just make out a small hole in the side of the bank.

'I'd show it to you,' said Pangali, 'but there wouldn't be room.' He eyed both of the children and then looked his own small body up and down. 'You just wouldn't fit.'

Kiri and Jed were keen to be off, but Pangali had to have breakfast first and once again both of them felt obliged to swallow a small shrimp each from the pile of grotesque wriggly bugs and beetles, worms and frogs.

'Hmm, delicious,' they both managed through gritted teeth. Pangali smiled with pleasure.

Finally, they set off, clambering by the side of the river, while Pangali plunged effortlessly through the water beside them. They walked on and on, stopping twice to rest while the sun rose high in the sky. Sweat began to drip from Kiri's skin. She looked at Jed and he looked hot too. Because of the heat and lack of sleep and food, the children soon became lost in a daydream state, slowly putting one foot in front of the other, aware of nothing else around them. Because of this, they took a moment to notice that Pangali was urgently signalling them.

'The apes!' he cried. 'The apes are coming. Jump into the river so they can't see you.'

'What?' said Kiri from her daze.

'Come on,' said Jed, dragging her into the water after him.

The cool water was like a slap to Kiri's face, and she rose to the surface of the river alert, her heart hammering. The children began to swim frantically, following the sleek form of Pangali ahead. For a long time the sound of the apes screaming ferociously assaulted the senses of Kiri and Jed every time they came up for air. Pangali the platypus urged them to continue swimming.

'Hurry,' he said, more than once. 'And don't look back – it will only slow you down.'

So they swam and swam until the two children felt they could swim no more. Even Kiri, who had loved water all of her life, could feel her lungs burning and her muscles aching from the frantic effort. More than once she considered getting out of the water and running along the bank – but there was no cover, and the apes would be sure to see her. So on they swam until suddenly Pangali held up a webbed limb. 'We can stop here. If you go up the hill straight ahead, there is a cave you can hide in. You must rest. I'll whistle to you when it is safe to come out.'

Jed looked up at the hill the platypus was waving towards. It was covered in thick bush. 'I can't see a cave,' he said.

'The birds tell me that it is straight ahead covered in bush. I'm sure you'll be able to find it when you get up there.'

'I hope the birds are right.'

'Of course!' Pangali sounded shocked. 'They are very truthful birds. They would never tell me anything that was a falsehood.'

In the background they could hear the cries of the apes. Kiri quickly dragged herself out of the river and reached to offer her hand to Jed.

'Where will you be, Pangali?' she said, helping Jed out of the river.

'I've got another burrow close by. The apes will never find it. Even another platypus would have trouble finding it, I'm sure. I'll keep my ears alert and I'll whistle when the coast is clear.'

The shouts were getting closer. It sounded like the apes were about to leap through the dense undergrowth at them.

'Run!' cried Pangali.

He disappeared into the river without his usual flourish. The children fled up the hill. They could hear the apes very close to them, catching up the distance with formidable speed.

'I can't see anything. I can't see a cave,' said Jed, scrambling through the bush ahead.

'Hang on a moment,' said Kiri. 'What's this?'

She pushed through a tight huddle of plants that Jed had just passed and found herself falling into darkness. The entrance was almost perfectly camouflaged.

'Jed,' she shouted cautiously. 'I'm down here.'

The apes sounded like they were almost on top of her and for a moment, her heart thudding, all she could hear were their wild cries. Then there was a whoosh and Jed landed in a ball at her feet. They felt the earth tremble when the apes charged overhead. Dirt showered from the ceiling and for several moments they both held their breath. Then there was silence. They sat quietly, straining their ears for any sound.

Kiri clutched her left ankle. It had taken the brunt of her fall.

'Is your ankle okay?' asked Jed.

Kiri stood up and tentatively put some weight on it. 'Yes. I think so.' Then after a time, she added, 'So what do we do now?'

'Wait for Pangali,' said Jed.

They waited. And waited. The darkness and stillness seemed to stretch into infinity.

'Do you think we should go and have a look?' whispered Kiri finally.

'No. Let's just wait.' Almost immediately they heard a loud piercing whistle.

'That must be Pangali,' whispered Jed.

'But what if it is one of the apes?' said Kiri, suddenly fearful again.

A loud piercing whistle ruptured the air again. 'It has to be Pangali,' said Jed, standing and peering out of the cave. 'Everything looks all right to me. Let's go.'

They climbed out of the small cave and made their way through the dense bush until they could see Pangali waving at them from the river. Kiri ran towards him and flopped herself down on the ground so that she was at eye level with him.

'Thanks for saving us, Pangali,' she said. 'Without you, the apes would have got us for sure.' She crinkled her nose. 'And I don't know what would have happened then!'

'You were wonderful, Pangali,' said Jed, sitting on the ground by Kiri. 'You are *the* platypus, dude!'

Pangali looked abashed. 'Really, it was nothing. Nothing at all.' He cleared his throat and changed the subject. 'So do you want to continue?' he asked. 'The pathway to the mine should be just past the cave you were in.'

'Really?' said Jed, turning around. 'You mean just up there?'

'Yes, the birds said to me ages ago that the pathway was near the cave. Once you have found it you can follow it to the mine. I'll just wait here for you,' said Pangali. 'I think I might go and get something more to eat. Would you like anything?'

'No thanks, Pangali,' said Kiri, hastily. 'We'll go and get our friends and we'll be back as soon as we can.'

Pangali gave them a small wave before he dived into the river. Jed and Kiri retraced their steps to the cave and then began walking around the cave in ever-widening circles. The sun blazed while they stumbled over the bush. It began to dip when they came to the conclusion that there was no pathway there.

'There's nothing here,' said Jed, eventually.

Kiri sighed with frustration. 'Let's go back to the river.'

They made their way to the river and were greeted by the smiling face of Pangali. 'Did you find them? Did you find the mine? Did you find your friends?'

'Um. There wasn't a path,' said Jed. 'We must have to go

further towards Black Mountain.'

'Oh, we can't do that!' Pangali sounded worried. 'We're getting too close as it is. That's where the giant lives and he's been making more noise than usual lately. I think it's much too dangerous to go any further. And when you get nearer to the mountain, it is pitch black even in the middle of the day, so it will be much too dangerous.'

'But we have to find the mine!' said Kiri, urgently. 'You said to follow the river towards Black Mountain until we find a path, so that's what we need to do.'

Jed suddenly whispered in Kiri's ear. After hearing what he had to say, she nodded enthusiastically.

'Come on Pangali,' said Jed. 'We should keep going. Besides, I think Kiri and I have something we need to do for you.'

'Do for me?'

'We can unblock the river for you, so you can swim home.'

For a moment Pangali could only stare at them with wide-open eyes, his beak slightly ajar.

'I think we'd have a much better chance unblocking the river than you would as a platypus,' said Kiri in a babble. 'Look, we have arms and legs and can lift things which you would find too heavy, and we can be on the ground, or in the water, when we are doing this–'

'You would do this for me?' whispered Pangali. 'You'd help me go home?'

'Oh, of course we would,' cried Kiri, and she leant into the water to touch one of his webbed limbs.

Pangali hid his beaked head in his webbed arms for a moment and they heard him gently sob. Jed stared at his feet looking uncomfortable, while Kiri patted Pangali's head. 'There, there, it'll be all right.'

For a time the platypus sobbed and Kiri did her best to comfort him until finally he had some composure back.

'Sorry, dear children,' he eventually managed to say. 'But to see my family again – just the thought of it is a dream come true.'

'We'd best get going then,' said Jed, jumping to his feet. 'I suggest we walk beside the river, as there are no apes around at the moment. Pangali, you can lead the way.'

'Excellent idea!' said Pangali, who dived into the water with a half somersault.

Jed and Kiri walked on, following the energetic form of Pangali while he swam.

'This is a really nice idea of yours,' said Kiri.

Jed shrugged. 'I just hope we can remove those rocks so he can go home after all of this. But in the meantime, keep your eyes alert for the pathway to the mine.'

Although it was the middle of the afternoon, when they pushed on further, they quickly found the light fading as Black Mountain loomed up overhead. When they had been stumbling around in the dark for the best part of an hour, following Pangali's now eager whistling and calling ('Come on, we're almost there! Almost there!'), Kiri tripped over a tree root and went crashing to the ground.

'Ouch,' she said, rolling on to her back, cradling her knee.

'Are you all right?' Jed gave her a hand up. 'First it was your hand, then your ankle, now your knee. Talk about being in the wars!'

'I'm fine! I'm tougher than I look.'

It was so dark now that they couldn't see each other, not even the whites of each other's eyes.

'Pangali, are we almost there?' Jed flicked the lighter on his Swiss army knife and held it in the air. The landscape around them was barren of life. There were dead trees and roots, and the river had disappeared to a thin black trickle. He picked up a piece of wood and tried to light it but it wouldn't catch because it was too wet. He flicked the lighter off and they stood together in the dark.

'He can't be far away,' said Kiri. 'Pangali! Pangali!'

Suddenly the most terrible skin-crawling sensation came over Kiri. Something that felt slightly sticky but furry brushed her arm and she had the feeling of a massive weight hovering just over her head.

'Je-e-e-d,' she said in a slow, panicked voice. Jed flicked the lighter on and Kiri looked up in horror at the underbelly of a large many-legged creature who had walked right over her and who was now rearing up over Jed. It had a red body with orange legs and head. The front legs, shaped like fangs, were poised to attack.

The creature hissed and then lunged at Jed. Jed scrambled back, dropping his lighter. Kiri felt around on the ground for a piece of wood, anything she could use for a weapon. She felt something solid in her hand and picked it up. She couldn't see anything, but the creature was hissing and making sucking noises, and she could hear Jed gasping and the thump of his body crashing to the ground and being tossed about. Then there was a shard of light as Jed found the lighter and flicked it on again. With the wood in her hand, Kiri hit the creature as hard as she could. A section of one of the creature's legs collapsed with the impact and the creature howled in pain. She saw Jed on the ground desperately grappling with his Swiss army knife, plunging it up into the creature's body, then everything was pitch black again. There was a terrible howl from the creature, much worse than the first cry, and then utter silence.

'Jed? Jed!'

She heard rustling and grunting and then a sound of something landing with a thud. She edged closer, her hands ready to swing the wood again. Then there was light again and she could see Jed pulling himself up, while the large creature lay on its back, quivering slightly. Its many slimy legs convulsed and then abruptly stilled. Jed slowly got to his feet. He appeared to be covered in grey slime and he stunk, but regardless Kiri was delighted to see him in one piece and broke into an uncontrollable smile. Then she looked around. Several other large, many-legged creatures were disappearing up the slope of the mountain. She looked back at Jed fearfully while he tried to wipe himself down.

'Biggest centipede I've ever seen, but at least the others are moving away from us,' Jed reassured Kiri with a wink, trying to look nonchalant on the outside, even though she could see that his hands were shaking.

'Where's Pangali gone?' He started to shout, 'Pangali! Pangali!' and Kiri joined in the chorus. Jed flicked his lighter on and off as they looked up and down the river frantically.

'Where's he gone?'

For a moment the thought of being stuck in the darkness was almost more than Kiri could bear. She wasn't a timid girl, but being at the base of Black Mountain would test the nerves of even the biggest and bravest of grown-ups. She bit her bottom lip and was about to suggest to Jed that they turn around when there was wild splashing and shouting from the water.

Pangali emerged from beneath the water, chattering excitedly. 'It's just around the next bend. There it is – all the rocks that are blocking the river. Come on children. Come on! Let's get me home.'

With Jed flicking his lighter on and off every now and then, they followed Pangali as quickly as they could along the treacherous dark surface. They turned the bend and there in front of them was a massive pile of large stones, each rock the size of an enormous boulder.

'Go ahead!' shouted Pangali with glee. 'I see how strong you are! Make me a path out of here and then I can go home!'

Jed and Kiri turned to look at each other, almost unable to bear the eager light in Pangali's eye. They couldn't move these. They had been expecting rocks or stones, not enormous boulders that were bigger than they were. What were they going to do?

Chapter 8

Climbing Black Mountain and meeting Olaf the Giant

K iri gaped at the enormous pile of rocks that blocked the river and then stared back at Pangali's enthusiastic face, her spirits plunging.

'We can't lift these by ourselves,' Jed said to the platypus, breaking the silence. Pangali's face instantly dropped and his brown eyes began to fill with tears. 'But don't worry; we're going to get help. You will go home.'

'Help?' whispered Kiri. 'What help?'

'We're going up into the mountain and we're going to get the giant to help us.'

'What!' said Kiri.

'Oh no! You can't do that!' said Pangali. 'The giant is

wicked. He isn't to be trusted. He won't help you.'

Jed debated back and forth for several minutes with Pangali until Kiri interjected. She couldn't bear to see the sadness in Pangali's eyes and the more she thought about Jed's idea, the more she thought it was better than not doing anything. 'Pangali, let's give this a go. Really, when I think about it, there's nothing to lose. The worst that the giant can say is no. But he could very well say yes, and I'm sure a giant is strong enough to lift these rocks.'

Pangali was quiet for a moment and then he sighed. 'Oh, I would love to see my family again,' he said in a wistful voice.

'It's all decided then!' said Jed. 'Perhaps you might like to go and have a rest. We might be a while finding the giant, but we'll be back as soon as we can.'

Jed flicked on his lighter and began marching up the hill before the platypus could begin debating the issue again. Kiri stared around her, scanning for any red and orange centipede creatures, and followed. She was careful where she put her feet as she followed Jed's gunky form.

'Thank you, dear children,' cried Pangali, and then there was a splash and he was gone.

Kiri caught up with Jed and they carefully and steadily began to ascend the mountain. They found a pathway of sorts, but it seemed it hadn't been used for a long time, because it was overgrown with dead vines. Still, it was better than climbing the rocks. Kiri constantly scanned the landscape for giant centipedes but decided she didn't want to discuss her fears of another attack with Jed – and she also decided not to tell Jed that he stunk. The centipede gunk on Jed smelt revolting. It was a stinky mixture like rotten apples and dog poo.

They walked on in silence, picking their way through the dead branches and vines that covered the pathway. Every so often Kiri could make out the form of a giant centipede moving in the shadows and she shuddered.

Unexpectedly the lighter went out and Kiri gave a small gasp of fright. She could hear Jed flicking the lighter several times. The darkness was so black she couldn't see anything at all. Not even a shadow of his outline.

'Sorry Kiri, but the lighter must have run out of fuel,' Jed said eventually.

'Now what are we going to do? I can't see a thing.'

'Neither can I.'

'Perhaps we should go back.'

'I think we should carry on. We have been climbing for so long we must be almost there. Besides, I don't want to let Pangali down.'

Kiri remembered Pangali's warm wet eyes and sighed. She gingerly stepped towards Jed, her arms outstretched, trying to find him. Eventually she felt the form of his slimy arm.

'Ah. I think you should hold my hand,' said Jed. 'We don't want to get separated from each other or we'll be in trouble.'

'Um.' Kiri thought about it for a moment. The circumstances were a little unusual. 'Okay.' She put her hand into his. 'Yuck, your hand is all slimy.'

'Sorry. That centipede stuff is revolting. I think I probably smell too.'

'Just a little,' said Kiri, not wanting to be too unkind.

Without light they stumbled slowly up the path, pausing often to feel their way through parts there were overgrown, then inexplicably the path became smooth and they no longer had to struggle through old dead vines.

'I think we must be getting there,' said Jed confidently – and when they turned the next bend they could make out the faraway light of a small hut. Kiri promptly let go of Jed's hand. With the light from the hut they could now make out the dim shadows of the rocks around them.

The small hut became larger and larger as they climbed towards it, until it was bigger than a small skyscraper and just as wide. When the children neared the door it towered over them. They stood by the large wooden door for a moment, both feeling nervous and fearful.

'We must be crazy,' whispered Kiri. 'They say he's violent.'

'I'm sure everything will be fine. But if he looks mean, we'll run away,' whispered Jed with false bravado.

Jed banged on the door loudly. Nothing happened. He knocked again. Still nothing happened. The third time both of them banged on the door.

'Hello!' shouted Kiri. 'Is anyone there?'

There was the sound of movement inside the hut and the ground trembled as heavy footsteps slowly came crashing towards them. Kiri felt the blood drain from her face. It was hard to tell what colour Jed was under the centipede gunk. The door swung open and a terrifying loud voice said, 'Who dares knock on my door!'

The massive form of the giant stood before them and Kiri found she was staring up at his knee. He was wearing old, dirty cotton trousers that needed mending.

'WHO DARES KNOCK ON MY DOOR!'

Kiri tried to make out the giant's face against the backdrop of the light in the hut. The giant had a sinister expression on his large face. He looked mean and Kiri debated whether they should turn and run.

'Ah, I'm Jed and this is Kiri – and we just wanted to ask you for some help, sir,' Jed said before Kiri could find her voice.

'Help?' the giant's face softened and he looked comically perplexed. 'Help? It's been a long while since anyone asked for my help.'

He took three steps back into the room and sat down with a heavy thud on a chair. The hut shook and dust fell from the ceiling. The children inched into the room. The hut was filthy. On the tables were unwashed dishes and clutter. Thick dust covered everything. Kiri sneezed.

'We have a friend who's trying to get home,' said Jed. 'We need your help to move some rocks.'

The giant sighed loudly, pulled out a large white handkerchief and blew his nose noisily.

'It's no good asking for my help,' he said eventually. 'I'm no good for anything. I'm useless. Utterly useless.'

'No, you're not!' said Kiri.

She inched closer to him and peered up into his face. He had the biggest and fattest nose she had ever seen and for a moment she was distracted by it, but then she noticed his eyes, moist with self-pity, and her heart melted.

'You're not useless! You shouldn't say things like that about yourself!'

The giant leant forward in his chair and looked at Kiri closely. She smiled nervously at him, suddenly alarmed by his large face looking down at her.

He sighed again. 'I am useless. Everyone gave up on me years ago. The wicked Chief stole the Jewel Egg and I couldn't even stop him – and he's not much bigger than you. See, for a giant I'm useless.'

Kiri fought hard to not step back – his breath was very bad – and put on her most sympathetic face. 'The Chief's horrible. He's a bad person. You can't help it if he stole the Jewel Egg.'

'But it was my job to guard it. And I was asleep when they attacked and before I knew it, it was gone.' He sighed again. 'I am useless.'

'Excuse me, sir.' Jed cleared his throat and the giant turned his head slowly to look at him. 'Can I point out that you are a giant and that you're really strong.'

'Strong?' The giant lifted his arm and flexed his muscles. His arm bulged. 'I suppose I am.' His arm fell limply to his side. 'But it's no good being strong when you're useless. It didn't help me defend myself against the Chief's monkey mob.'

'But sir, you could use your strength right now and be useful.'

The giant stared at Jed for what felt like ages, but was really only a second or two. 'How?' he said finally, adjusting the braces that held up his cotton trousers.

'Our friend is a platypus and he lives in the river. There are some rocks in the river that are blocking his path. If you could lift the rocks out of the river he would be able to swim home.'

The giant frowned. 'I suppose I could lift some rocks.'

'Of course you can!' said Kiri. 'You're very strong.'

'I suppose if I lift some rocks it will help your friend?'

'Of course it will,' said Jed. 'He'll be able to go home.'

'It's no good though,' said the giant with another great sigh. 'I have to stay here.'

'Why?'

'It's my job.'

'I thought your job was to guard the Jewel Egg?' said Jed.

'It is.'

'But it was stolen, so you don't need to stay here anymore.'

The giant was silent for a moment and then his face cleared into a big smile. 'You're right! I don't need to stay here any more.' He rose to his feet. 'Show me where the rocks are and I will lift them for you!'

It took a while to explain that the river was down the mountain, and then it took some time for the giant to find a lamp that worked to take with him, and when they finally set off it also took a moment for the giant to realise that the children couldn't keep up with his gigantic strides.

'How about I carry you?' he asked eventually.

Kiri stared at his enormous hands and had an unnerving vision of them accidentally squeezing the breath out of her body. 'That might be difficult for you, but how about we climb on your back? That way we could hold on to your braces.'

'Okay.' The giant knelt down and the children climbed up each side of his back and clung on as he rose metres into the air. Kiri let out a gasp of exhilaration. It was better than any roller coaster she'd ever been on.

'My name is Olaf,' said the giant conversationally while he crashed down the mountain in long strides.

'It's nice to meet you, Olaf,' said Kiri sincerely and Olaf beamed a large smile.

'Nice to meet you,' he muttered to himself. 'Now that has a nice ring to it, doesn't it? Nice to meet you.' He sniffed suddenly. 'What's that funny smell? It's sort of like rotten apples and–'

'Um, that's Jed. He was attacked by a giant centipede.'

'I think it's some sort of gunk they secrete,' said Jed.

'Giant centipedes? Goodness me. Are they bigger than me?'

'Oh no! But they are bigger than us.'

'Oh.' Olaf sounded disappointed. 'That's a shame really. I like the idea of them being bigger. It can be difficult when everyone else is so small. You see no one really understands what it is like to be as big as me. It's not easy being big.'

The children couldn't think of anything to say in the face of Olaf's self-pity so they continued the rest of the journey down the mountain in silence until they heard the sound of the river.

'We're almost there!' said Kiri.

'Straight ahead, Olaf!' said Jed.

The giant crossed the remaining ground quickly and before they knew it they were clambering off Olaf's back on to the side of the river. Olaf set his lamp down on a nearby rock and looked at the river curiously.

'This isn't right,' he said. 'The water isn't flowing. It's down to a little trickle.'

'The rocks are in the way,' said Kiri gently, pointing to the pile to the giant's right.

'Oh, the rocks. Of course. I'd forgotten about them.'

'Pangali! Pangali! We're back,' shouted Kiri.

'Who's Pangali?' asked Olaf.

'The platypus we were telling you about,' said Jed.

'Oh. Of course.'

At that moment Pangali's head peered at them out of the water, his big eyes looking at the giant fearfully.

Kiri bent down to greet him. 'We're back, and look – we brought the giant with us.'

'I can see that,' whispered Pangali. 'But is he safe?'

'Oh yes, he's quite harmless, and he's agreed to lift the rocks for us.'

Pangali's eyes narrowed. 'Did he say what he wanted for doing that? Giants are mean, you know. They aren't going to do something for nothing.'

There was a loud grunt, a splash and the sound of a shriek. Pangali disappeared under the water in fear. Kiri turned around in alarm to see Jed's spluttering form emerging from the water.

'Hey!'
Jed shouted at the giant from the river.
'What did you do that for?'

'You smelt. It was putting me off,' said Olaf, striding into the river.

He offered Jed his hand. Jed looked at it thoughtfully before accepting and Olaf helped him back on to the riverbank.

Olaf sniffed the air noisily. 'That's much better.'

Pangali's face bobbed out of the water. 'Psst.' He caught Kiri's attention. 'Look at that! Now do you see what I mean! The giant's evil. We are doomed. He's probably planning to kill us off one by one. We must flee! Flee!'

'Don't be silly,' said Kiri. 'Olaf was just helping Jed clean up. He did smell revolting. And look, he's even helping him dry off.'

From a pocket somewhere, the giant had found a clean handkerchief (at least Kiri hoped it was clean) and was now on his knees encasing Jed in it like he was a little puppy. Within a minute, instead of being wet and dripping, Jed was damp and ruffled.

'Ah, thanks,' said Jed, in a somewhat dubious voice, while the giant rose to his feet.

'Who's that in the water?' Olaf asked in a suddenly suspicious voice. In a stride he was by Kiri's side peering down into the water.

'It's Pangali, the platypus,' said Kiri.

'Platypus,' said Olaf.

He reached into the water and plucked the unhappy creature into the air. Pangali closed his eyes as he was hurtled metres up high.

'What an odd-looking creature,' said Olaf, peering at him. 'He's furry and warm, with a beak like a duck. It's like several creatures cobbled together into one. How odd.'

Pangali opened his eyes, looked up the giant's nostrils

and quickly closed them again. 'Would you mind putting me down,' he demanded. 'And I am not odd. I think you're odd.'

'Oh.' The giant looked crestfallen. 'You think I'm odd.'

His voice sounded so sad that Pangali opened his eyes again and peered at him for a moment.

'Well, not that odd,' he said finally. 'But how about you put me back into the water and I'll have a think about it.'

'Okay.'

The giant gently lowered Pangali into the water. The platypus dived into the river before surfacing with a small flourish.

'No, you're not at all odd for a giant!' he shouted at the giant, who beamed from ear to ear.

'Although, I still say he might be planning to kill us off one at a time,' he whispered to Kiri.

The giant strode into the river with a look of satisfaction on his face and picked up the nearest boulder like it was a tennis ball and threw it on to the riverbank. The ground vibrated and Kiri involuntarily screamed.

'Olaf, you probably want to put the rocks down slowly. Um, throwing them around is a bit dangerous,' said Jed in a diplomatic voice.

'Oh. Okay.'

The giant began to work, methodically lifting boulders and carefully placing them on the riverbank. The pile in the river quickly became a mini mountain on the riverbank. As the water began to flow, Pangali's eyes opened wider and wider in astonishment and excitement. Finally, Olaf stepped on to the bank and sat down, breathing heavily.

'All done,' he said, panting.

'Oh, Pangali!' cried Kiri. 'You'll be able to go home! This is wonderful news.'

'I really don't know what to say,' said Pangali. 'I'm so happy. I'm finally going to see my family again!'

For a time, there were hugs and kisses and some tears shed, mainly by Pangali, while the children said goodbye to the platypus.

'Thank you, kind giant,' Pangali said, before he dived into the water to begin his journey home. They watched his little bobbing form rising in and out of the water.

'Good luck with finding the mine,' he shouted from a distance before disappearing from view.

Olaf the Giant suddenly began to weep loudly, huge tears falling down his face and landing with a splash on the ground where he sat.

'What's the matter?' cried Jed and Kiri at the same time. But for ages all the giant could do was sit there and cry.

'What on earth is wrong with him?' said Jed to Kiri. 'I didn't think he was that attached to Pangali. He can't be.

He's only just met him.'

The giant began dabbing his eyes with the handkerchief that he had used to dry Jed.

'I miss Daisy!' Olaf suddenly wailed.

'Who's Daisy?' asked Kiri.

'My wife. The wicked Chief took her away.'

Jed and Kiri exchanged looks.

'He has a wife?' said Jed in disbelief. 'But he's so ugly.'

'We'll find the mine, and then we'll help him find Daisy,' said Kiri at the same time.

Chapter 9

The Attempt to Rescue Daisy

There was something very disturbing about witnessing a giant cry. Not only was it a noisy business, but his tears were beginning to create a pool and his sobs made the ground shake.

'It's okay. It'll be all right,' soothed Kiri, standing on tiptoes to pat Olaf's knee.

'They took my precious Daisy and I don't know where she is,' was all that Olaf could say over and over while he continued to shed large tears. They pleaded and cajoled with the giant to calm down until finally he wrung out his handkerchief several times, took a deep breath and sat up still and quiet.

'We know where Daisy is,' said Kiri, now that the giant was calm enough to hear what she was saying. 'She's locked in the Chief's dungeon. She was wearing a, ah, lovely floral sundress when we saw her. We'll help you get her back.'

'Do we really want to do that?' Jed whispered to Kiri.

'Of course we do! If we can help Pangali, we can help Olaf. We might as well make ourselves useful while we try to find the mine,' Kiri whispered back.

'Yes, of course, you're right. Sorry. Just the shock that he's got a wife has thrown me.'

Olaf wasn't listening to their muttered conversation. Instead a big smile spread slowly over his large face. 'That is what she was wearing the day they captured her and took her away. How was my lovely? How did she look?'

Jed made a face that Olaf didn't notice, while Kiri said, 'She was sleeping peacefully when we saw her.'

'Oh, that's so wonderful. She always looks beautiful, and I always used to love watching her sleep.'

Jed made an even larger face and Kiri poked him in the ribs. The giant hadn't seen, however, and his face was suddenly downcast.

'It's no good,' he muttered. 'I can't leave the mountain to get her.'

'Why ever not?'

'Because I have to guard the Jewel Egg.'

'Um, I think we've been over this,' said Jed, rolling his eyes. 'The Jewel Egg has been stolen, so there is no need for you to stay. It was no problem coming down the mountain, was it?'

The giant's large ugly face cleared. 'Yes, you're right. We can go and rescue Daisy.'

'I hope you have a plan,' said a little voice at their feet and they all jumped at the sound.

'A good plan, a good plan,' chirped another little voice.

Almost like one person, Olaf, Jed and Kiri turned and peered at the small figures that had suddenly appeared and were now standing on a little rock. They were two bird-like creatures wearing bow ties. They had brilliantly coloured wings that kept changing hue from blue to purple to red to pink to orange to yellow to green and back to blue again. They both had a bright red mop of hair.

'Allow me to introduce myself,' said the slightly larger one. Kiri noticed then he was wearing a black bow tie. 'My name is Big Wig Knockulous.' He bowed with a flourish. 'And my companion here is Wee Wig Knockulous.' He gestured to his friend, who was slightly smaller and who wore a yellow polka dot bow tie.

'A pleasure, a pleasure!' chirped Wee Wig Knockulous, bobbing up and down with enthusiasm.

'Goodness, they're birds,' said Kiri.

'They're knockulouses!' said the giant sounding very surprised. 'I haven't seen them in these parts for years!'

'Oh, hello!' said Kiri and she proceeded to make introductions for herself, Jed and Olaf. The giant peered at the knockulouses more closely and sniffed at the air directly in front of them.

'Would you mind giving us some space!' said Big Wig Knockulous in a stiff voice, waving Olaf away with his wing.

'Oh, sorry.' The giant sat back bashfully. 'I'm most sorry. You just smell different …

I mean nice.'

'That will be the new cologne,' said Big Wig Knockulous with a smile.

'Cologne?' said Jed.

'Perfume,' confirmed Big Wig.

'You wear perfume?' said Jed.

'What's wrong with that?'
said Big Wig.

'Nothing, ah … nothing. Just the birds back home don't do that.'

'Birds? We're not just mere birds. Like the giant said, we are knockulouses,' said Big Wig, standing up proudly. 'And we just happened to overhear your conversation and thought we might be able to be of assistance to you – especially as you were talking about visiting the mine.'

'The mine! The mine!' squeaked Wee Wig.

'Quite,' said Big Wig. 'The thing is, if you are seeking the mine, well, dear chaps, you are currently going in the wrong direction.'

'But Pangali said it was towards Black Mountain,' said Kiri.

'Oh dear, trust a platypus to send you the wrong way,' said Big Wig. 'They aren't known for their sense of direction, although they do mean well. You have to travel *away* from Black Mountain to find the path. It's not far from where the tyrant Chief Namba lives. Nasty, traitorous man.'

'Can you really take us there?' asked Kiri.

'We would be delighted to show you the way,' said Big Wig. 'But I just have one question first – why do you want to go there? It's a dreadful place devoid of light, many metres below the surface, guarded by the Chief's apes. Only someone with a death wish would go there. We don't advise a visit.'

'Our friends are there. We have to rescue them,' said Kiri.

'It's very dangerous,' said Big Wig in a serious voice. 'You would be risking life and limb. There is little chance of success. No child has ever come out of that mine alive.'

'We have to save them or at least try,' said Kiri equally as firmly.

Big Wig Knockulous bowed slowly and Wee Wig Knockulous followed his example, although he bent over too far, banged his head on the ground and stood up again looking dizzy.

'It is an honour to meet you, dark maiden,' Big Wig said gravely. 'You are a brave heroine to take on a task so dangerous in an effort to try and save your friends.'

Kiri was quiet for some time. The praise was unexpected; she really didn't know what to say. As far as she was concerned she was just an ordinary girl trying to do the best thing in a bad situation.

Big Wig Knockulous broke the growing silence. 'We will take you to your friends then.'

'How are we going to rescue them?' said Jed. 'We've come up against the apes before and only just got away in one piece.'

'I'll help,' said Olaf, who had been listening to the conversation with his mouth slightly open. 'First we'll get my Daisy and then we'll get your friends.'

'Very good!' Big Wig rose in the air for a moment, and Wee Wig jumped up and down excitedly. 'Two giants are always better than one and will give us some brute strength in our endeavours. Wee Wig and I can lead the way and we can also act as scouts. Let the mission to the mine begin!'

So that is how Kiri and Jed came to be travelling through the countryside on the back of a giant who was carrying a large lamp, with two brightly coloured bird-like creatures fluttering around their heads. Wee Wig Knockulous kept staring at Kiri like a love-struck teenager and Big Wig had to keep telling him to behave himself.

'A mission! A mission!' Wee Wig kept chirping to himself happily. 'Yippee! Yippee!'

Slowly the landscape changed from dark and mountainous to tropical green forests and lush grass. Olaf's lamp began to die, but now there was natural light they didn't need it any more. When it had completely burnt out he placed it beside an irregularly shaped rock.

'What a shame the light has run out,' he said wistfully. 'Daisy doesn't like the dark. She's scared of it.'

Kiri pondered this new information about Daisy being scared of the dark even though she was a giant, and onward the strange assortment of travelling companions moved, the ground trembling beneath the giant's footsteps while the air fluttered with the knockulouses.

Jed's stomach growled loudly with hunger. 'I'd give anything for a big, chunky meat burger with all the trimmings right now,' he muttered. 'Or on second thoughts a bowl of French fries, smothered with tomato sauce ... or then again, perhaps a gooey raspberry sundae.'

'Don't say anything more. You're making me hungrier than I already am,' said Kiri.

They passed the beach they had first landed at, and Kiri contemplated for a moment how much had happened since they had first arrived. Kiri remembered the timetable in her pocket and hoped they would soon be taking the return Elastic Island service home. The giant increased his pace and the knockulouses began to pant trying to keep up in the sky.

'Slow down! Slow down!' squeaked Wee Wig Knockulous.

'I think we should stop and formulate a plan,' suggested Big Wig Knockulous loudly.

'I agree,' said Jed. 'A game plan is crucial.'

'My Daisy is up there,' said Olaf, pointing now at the imposing castle that stood at the top of the long pathway. He started walking even faster, the ground shuddering under his weight. The children clung on to his braces desperately.

'Stop! Stop!' cried Wee Wig.

'Giant, we need a plan! Let's stop and discuss this rationally for a moment,' shouted Big Wig.

'Daisy! Daisy!' the giant cried, almost breaking into a run as the castle loomed closer.

'Look, giant, we really need a plan otherwise bad things may happen–'

At Big Wig's words there were the terrible shrieking sounds of the Chief's apes descending from behind rocks like a swarm of big, black flies.

'Arghhh!' roared Olaf in a loud, threatening voice.

He bent down and with the back of his hand knocked a dozen apes to the ground.

'Go Olaf!' shouted Kiri in encouragement.

Olaf turned and with another sweep of his hand knocked another twenty apes to the ground. 'Daisy!' he cried. 'Daisy!'

'Watch out behind you!' said Jed in alarm. A band of apes was attacking the giant's feet and legs with long spears.

'Ouch!' Olaf shook one foot, sending apes flying.

He put his foot back down, crushing several other apes in the process. A lone ape suddenly came from behind a rock and darted at his exposed ankle, plunging a long arrow into it, before escaping back behind a rock. As the ape fled he let out a loud wail and then all the apes began retreating.

'We're winning!' shouted Jed happily.

'I don't feel so good,' said Olaf, teetering unsteadily on his feet. 'I feel funny.'

'What's happening?' said Kiri.

'Oops. I think I spoke too soon. I don't like the look of this,' said Jed, while they swayed dangerously from side to side.

Kiri looked up and around for the knockulouses, but they seemed to have disappeared. The giant staggered about and then suddenly his legs gave out from underneath him. He crashed to the ground like a toppled tree and the children flung themselves away from him as he hit the earth, rolling on to the stony path. Immediately apes leapt from behind the rocks, pinning a squirming Kiri and slightly dazed Jed, overcoming them in seconds. Kiri stared at Olaf in despair.

'They've killed him!' she cried.

'No, it's all right,' said Jed. 'Look – he's breathing.'

Sure enough, when Kiri looked again, there was a rhythmic rise and fall of the giant's chest.

'Oh, thank goodness,' she muttered.

The children watched helplessly while the apes wrapped ropes around the slumbering giant that they then attached to large logs, creating a rough sort of stretcher. Shrieking and jabbering they hauled the giant up to the castle, dragging the children along behind them.

When they entered through the castle gates Chief Namba stood in his exotic finery, wearing a green trouser-skirt, and emerald and bone necklace. The tiny monkey at his feet was dressed in a matching emerald waistcoat and straw hat. The monkey clapped his hands enthusiastically.

'Well done,' the Chief said to one of the apes – presumably one of the apes in charge – and the creature puffed out his chest importantly. Chief Namba glanced at the slumbering form of the giant. 'Put the giant fool in the dungeon,' he said. 'In the cell next to his wife.'

Scores of apes struggled away with the giant and the Chief turned his fierce face to the two children.

'How dare you seek to escape from me! I order that you will be executed at sunrise. For now, throw them in the dungeon!'

The apes that held them began to jostle them away.

'I wouldn't do that if I were you!' said Kiri suddenly in a loud, forceful voice.

The Chief turned and waved the apes to stop. 'What did you say, child?'

'I am Kiri of the Land of the Long White Cloud, and this is Jed of the Land of the Long White Cloud. You wouldn't dare execute us! If you do there is no telling what will unfold because we are the interpreters of dreams.'

The Chief glared at them. 'I haven't had any dreams since your escape. I don't care that you interpret dreams. Besides I still have your friends in the mines if I need an interpreter.'

'Not only do we interpret dreams,' said Kiri like he hadn't spoken. 'We also dream our own dreams. Both of us have dreamed of the black panther in recent days. He is stalking though your palace, past your grounds and into the bush. It signifies danger to you and without us you will never know where this danger comes from and how to defend yourself against it. We can see your end coming – and without us there is nothing you can do about it.'

The Chief frowned, turned and walked to the steps of the castle. 'Take them to the dungeon,' he muttered to his commanding ape.

The children were roughly forced directly into a darkened cell through a door shaped like a mouth. They could barely see each other through the gloom.

'So what are we going to do now?' said Jed, sounding grumpy. 'And what was all that stuff about dreams and his evil days coming to an end?'

Kiri was quiet for a moment. 'I don't know what we're going to do,' she finally admitted. 'But I just have this strong feeling that it's all going to turn around tomorrow. I just wanted to make the Chief think we are people he needs to pay attention to, that's all.'

'I hope so,' muttered Jed. He took some straw in the corner and began scrunching it around to create a bed. 'I've had enough of this island. And I really don't want to be executed tomorrow. It's not my idea of a good way to start the day. Now bacon and eggs on toast I could cope with …'

Jed lay down on the straw and immediately fell into a deep sleep. Kiri sat a little away from him, her dark eyes blazing thoughtfully.

Chapter 10

The Awful Discovery of the Other Children in the Mines

Next morning Jed and Kiri were woken by the sound of the heavy door of their cell swinging open. Blurry-eyed they were shoved to their feet by two apes and marched into the pale morning light. Several mid-sized monkeys, wearing red waistcoats and straw hats, circled the group.

'What's going on?' said Jed.

'Where are you taking us?' asked Kiri.

Neither of them wanted to voice their ultimate nightmare – that they were being frogmarched to the execution site.

'I'm not going anywhere unless you tell me what's happening,' said Jed, putting his feet firmly on the ground. The ape grunted and manhandled him on with only a little more effort.

'I am Kiri of the Land of the Long White Cloud,' said Kiri in a loud voice, trying to sound as authoritative as possible. 'Stop now and tell us where we are going.'

There was an immediate hesitation, a certain nervousness that emanated from the two apes. They grunted at each other, and the monkeys went into a small huddle and muttered to each other in high voices.

'The mines,' one of the monkeys said after their short meeting. 'Your execution is delayed.'

'For now that is,' said another monkey, who began to laugh in a menacing high-pitched squeal. 'Enjoy your reprieve while you can – it won't last!'

The apes grunted and began manhandling the children along the courtyard again, towards the main gates.

'The mines,' whispered Jed across to Kiri, who nodded at him excitedly.

'They're taking us to Emma and Ethan!'

The apes carried them from the castle, then down the wide road with its curious large stones, before they turned off, near the river, on to a winding path that steadily grew narrower and narrower until they came to a deep mineshaft. The apes carried each child, slung unceremoniously on their backs, down a section of ladders. Just when Kiri thought they couldn't possibly go any lower they finally reached the bottom. The apes walked through a narrow tunnel that then opened into a large underground space. The apes dumped the children on the ground and pushed them forward. Kiri looked about them, searching for Emma in the midst of the activity, trying to adjust her eyes to the dim light.

It was a vast chamber, and all along the walls there were gangs of children slowly chipping away at the stone's surface with picks. Kiri couldn't see their faces, but they worked with a slow, monotonous apathy that was heartbreaking.

There was a large machine at the end of the chamber that clanked and crunched away. Into it children poured wheelbarrows of large rocks, and then out of the machine came a slowly moving conveyor belt of smaller rocks that had been crushed. At the beginning of the conveyor belt children were pouring grease over the crushed rocks, and for the rest of the belt children were picking out diamonds and sapphires and rubies and emeralds and other precious jewels. These they put in big buckets that apes carried away when full. Kiri couldn't see where the apes were taking the jewels.

The apes pushed them towards the conveyor belt and mimed that they needed to start picking for jewels. Refusing to be separated, Jed and Kiri managed to keep side by side. They began to work, and Kiri put her head down when one of the apes tried to indicate she should move further along the line. Finally, the apes seemed to decide the children were working at an acceptable pace, so they backed away and began to stroll around the chamber on sentry duty.

Kiri watched the small hands next to hers and copied their movements. Fortunately, it wasn't as hard as it looked.

The grease made the jewels easy to detach from the rock.

'Hi,' said Jed to the girl next to him, but she didn't respond. 'Hey you!' he said in a louder voice. Still there was no response. Jed turned to Kiri. 'They aren't very friendly.'

Kiri turned to the boy next to her. 'Hello, we're looking for our friends, Emma and Ethan.'

The boy didn't respond. He just carried on working.

'Can you hear me?'
said Kiri in a louder voice.

Still there was no response. Instinct made her reach out and touch the boy's arm. The boy turned and looked at her with obvious surprise. Like the other children he was covered in dust and dirt and he had long, unwashed hair down to his shoulders. His features were barely recognisable with all the grime, but he had the most amazing eyes Kiri had ever seen. They glowed luminous and vividly blue, more vibrant even than the jewels they were extracting from rock.

'Hello,' said Kiri. 'Have you seen our friends? A girl with blonde hair and a boy with red hair? They're both quite small.'

The boy stared at her mutely, clearly confused.

'My name is Kiri,' she said slowly, pointing to herself.

At that the boy frowned at her and then pointed to himself and made a guttural, indistinct noise.

An ape walked past, and they bent to their work again.

When he had passed by, Kiri whispered to Jed. 'I think he's deaf. What about the girl next to you?'

Jed nudged the girl next to him and she looked at him with annoyance. She had brilliant emerald green eyes. 'Can you hear me?' he said.

Her brow puckered, and she leant her head to one side.

'Can you hear me?' he repeated.

She frowned again, watching his lips move, then pulled her long hair back off her face with obvious irritation and returned to her work.

'Look!' hissed Kiri in horror, and only when Jed looked again did he see what had alarmed Kiri. The girl beside him didn't have any ears. There was just a small hole where each of her ears should have been. Kiri gazed around the table, desperately searching for any evidence of ears under the long matted hair of the children around them. And while she watched and people flicked hair out of their eyes, or scratched their head, or pulled up from putting a jewel into a bucket, it seemed that none of them had any.

'What's happened to them?' said Kiri.

'I don't know,' said Jed. 'But it can't be good.' Kiri and Jed worked until their fatigue threatened to overwhelm them. Their fingers began to cramp, and their backs hurt. Even their eyesight was beginning to dim, and it became harder and harder to see the dull jewels amid the stone and the grease. Then the monotony was broken by the clanging of a bell and all the children began to settle into small groups.

Apes walked around passing out buckets of water and dry bread. Kiri scanned the groups of children, frantically looking for the twins.

'Look! There they are,' she said, pointing at two small figures alone in a corner, their party finery now the colour of charcoal. They hurried towards them, but then Kiri caught sight of the children seated alongside the stone walls and swallowed. They were clearly blind, with their eyes closed like newborn kittens.

'Emma!' said Kiri, embracing her filthy, dirt-covered friend.

'Kiri! You're here!' gasped Emma.

'Am I so pleased to see you,' said Ethan to Jed.

'Don't worry, we're going to get you out,' said Kiri. 'But what's happened to the other children here?'

'I'm not sure. All I know is that all the children working on the conveyor belt don't have any ears. And those that work on the wall don't have any eyes,' said Emma.

'But how can that be?'

'Hmmm. Hmmm. Hhrppp.' There was the sound of someone clearing their throat and the children looked around with interest.

'Big Wig! Wee Wig!' cried Kiri, before turning to Emma and Ethan. 'These are knockulouses. They helped us find the mine.'

'We said we would. We said we would,' chirped Wee Wig happily, while Big Wig made a deep, elegant bow.

'What's happened to the children here?' said Kiri.

'Oh.' Big Wig and Wee Wig Knockulous exchanged sorrowful glances. 'It all started five years ago … dreadful Chief Namba–'

'Yes, he is dreadful, isn't he!' said Ethan.

'He is the evillest man in our land,' said Big Wig, shaking his red mop of hair. 'He did the most despicable, dastardly thing when he stole the Jewel Egg from Black Mountain and took Jewel Lagoon by force for his own evil ends. The beloved Princess Makana was forced to retreat to Free Bay and has no influence in these regions any more. It is a tragedy! Now in the Chief's mine these poor young children are forced to live their lives like this! And the Chief won't let them have their eyes or ears, depending on his mood. You will have seen firsthand how unstable the man is.'

'But that's awful!' cried Emma. Ethan had to whisper to her to hush when an ape looked angrily in their direction. 'That's terrible,' she whispered. 'But where are their parents? Why doesn't someone rescue them?'

'I'm sorry, dear child, but they are all orphans,' said Big Wig. 'Their parents were slaughtered on that dreadful day when the Chief seized power with his army of apes.'

Emma began to cry, long slow tears rolling from her eyes and down her cheeks. 'Those poor children!' She turned to Ethan. 'They're all orphans, just like Kiri. Gosh, I so miss

Mum and Dad. Do you?'

'Yes, I do,' Ethan said sincerely.

'We thought we'd lost you,' said Kiri to Big Wig.

'Yes, my dear girl. I am sorry that we had to leave when the apes captured you, but there was nothing we could do at that time to help you,' said Big Wig. 'However, we did manage to put a potion into the Chief's drink that has given him a frightful headache. He never misses an execution and I think it will be a few hours before he recovers, so we may have bought you a little time.'

'Headache! Headache!' squeaked Wee Wig. 'The Chief's got a headache!'

'Gosh, you're very clever!'
said Kiri.

Big Wig shook his head modestly. 'Really it was nothing,' he said.

'We need to get out of this place,' said Kiri, looking around her. 'What do you suggest, Big Wig?'

'Hmmm, let me think,' said Big Wig, rising gracefully into the air and sweeping the room. He circled twice, the second time as though double-checking an idea, and then he landed on the ground next to Wee Wig, who was hopping excitedly from one foot to another. The children looked at him expectantly.

'You need to make a distraction. I believe we're on

borrowed time at the moment, so you should target the next break. Notice that the apes are all in their own group over there? I suggest you sit at the other end of the mine next time, and then you can make a run for it.'

'But what sort of distraction should we make?' said Emma.

'I know!' said Ethan, before Big Wig could offer his ideas. He scuttled to a nearby rock and pulled out the battered blue backpack that he had hidden. 'I have a bomb!' He pulled out his alarm clock from the bag and sheltered it with his body so the apes wouldn't see it.

'Excellent idea,' said Jed, while Emma gasped.

'Don't worry, Em,' said Ethan. 'It isn't a big bomb. It'll just be a small explosion, nothing too major, but probably enough to get the apes worried.'

'I have to say, the bomb combined with the dive-bombing Wee Wig and I are planning to do will be perfect,' said Big Wig.

'Oh, dive-bombing!' said Wee Wig, fluttering his wigs. 'Oh goody!'

'How do you set this thing?' asked Jed.

Ethan began turning the different knobs and suddenly the mine was filled with the sounds of Hawaiian guitar music. 'Oh no! The radio,' Ethan muttered.

'Turn it off,' hissed Kiri.

'Oh!' gasped Emma when several of the apes began to rise

to their feet, looking around them.

With sweat falling from his face, Ethan turned another knob and the music came to an abrupt end. He carefully turned several other knobs, concentrating intensely while he did so. Kiri watched the apes carefully. They sat down again and then began slapping each other on the back, making noises like they were choking – but then she decided that they weren't choking after all, they appeared to be laughing at a joke.

'You won't be laughing soon,' Kiri said under her breath, turning back to the others. Ethan had finished fiddling and the clock was ticking with a deeper thud than before. 'We need to put that next to where the apes usually sit,' Kiri said.

Ethan looked over towards the menacing group and shook his head. 'I'm not taking it over there!'

'Then I will,' said Kiri and held out her hand for the alarm clock.

Ethan stared at her, looked at the group of apes and then stared at his homemade bomb.

'We want to create maximum effect – and it would be best if your bomb goes off by the apes. Besides we don't want any of the other children to be hurt,' said Kiri, still holding her hand out.

'She's right,' said Jed, elbowing Ethan, who looked once more at the group of apes and then back at Kiri before handing her the alarm clock. He made a face.

'What time did you set it for?' said Emma.

'It will go off in one hundred and twenty minutes. That's the next break.'

'Are you sure it'll go off then?'

Ethan simply gave her a look.

'Won't there be some apes guarding the top of the mine?' said Jed.

'No, we've checked all of that,' said Big Wig. 'The apes might be big, but they're a bit stupid. Every break they all gather in that group over there.'

There was the sound of the bell again, at which Kiri rose to her feet and slipped like a shadow towards the apes. They were breaking off into ones and twos and drifting with the flow of children back to the various work spaces in the mines. Kiri tried to melt against the rocks. One of the apes began to turn towards Kiri, but then he was slapped on the back by another ape and they fell into walking in line together away from Kiri. She darted behind a rock and placed the alarm clock bomb near were the apes had been sitting. She then walked quickly to a place on the conveyor belt by Emma.

'Oh Kiri!' gasped Emma in obvious admiration.

'Grrrrrhhh!' roared an ape marching past.

The children spent an anxious two hours methodically picking jewels from the rock, whispering words of encouragement to each other and looking towards the ladder that they would climb to freedom. If the plan worked, that was. The minutes slowly inched by and the tension in each of them began to build. Would their plan work?

Then the bell sounded and they began to huddle together, this time at the other side of the mine.

'It hasn't gone off yet,' hissed Kiri.

'It will,' said Ethan, who was busying himself emptying items from his pockets into his bag.

Then there was the sound of a small explosion and all mayhem broke loose. The alarm clock exploded, sending a cloud of dust and dirt into the air. Big Wig and Wee Wig began dive-bombing, and the children could hear the howls of the apes as the knockulouses made contact with their eyes. Some of the eyeless and earless children began to wail with fright.

'Come on,' cried Kiri as she raced towards the ladder.

The others followed, Emma dragging up the rear. 'But we can't leave the others,' she said, as if only just realising that they were leaving the other children to the same terrible fate they had already endured for five years.

'Come on,' said Ethan. 'Hurry up, Emma.' He grabbed his sister's arm and dragged her along. 'We can't do anything for them.'

'But we could try!'

Fear caused Emma to begin screaming. She screamed and screamed with a power that was astounding for someone so small, the noise triggering more wailing from the children of the mine who still had their ears. The sounds echoed around the chamber, causing further chaos to the apes, who were now covering their ears at the high-pitched sound while the knockulouses continued to dive-bomb them.

'Em, you have to stop screaming,' Ethan said to his sister while he continued to drag her towards the ladder. He turned and stared at her, before giving her a small shake. 'Pull yourself together!'

She became silent. 'Sorry,' she whispered.

Frantically they began climbing, up and up and up, ever fearful that suddenly an ape would come climbing after them, a hairy arm reaching out to grab a leg. It was with relief that they finally broke through the dark shaft to the light of day. They collapsed, panting on the ground in the mid-morning air. Big Wig and Wee Wig fluttered anxiously overhead as the children recovered their breath.

'Children, are you all right?' asked Big Wig.

'Oh oh, oh oh,' said Wee Wig.

'We need to get out of here,' said Jed, when he could finally speak.

'Let's head to the beach and hide until we can catch Elastic Island home again,' said Ethan, adjusting his backpack.

'We have to help the children down in the mine,' said Emma firmly. 'We can't just leave them there. Some of them have been trapped down there for five years. That's terrible.'

'There's nothing we can do,' said Ethan. 'We're lucky that we escaped.'

'Ethan, I think Emma's right. We can't just leave them,' said Jed. 'I don't know what we are going to do, though.'

'We need to go to the Chief's castle,' said Kiri suddenly.

Big Wig alighted on the ground in front of them. 'You need to get the Jewel Egg from the palace,' he said solemnly. 'You need to restore power back to its rightful place. That's the only way you can save the children down there.'

'That's all very well,' said Ethan. 'But there is no way the four of us can break into the castle and steal this egg thingy.'

'Jewel Egg,' corrected Kiri. 'And I know a way we can break in.'

'Really?' said Emma.

'And I know where we can get help once we are there.' She glanced at Jed. 'I think Olaf and Daisy will be very useful in this situation. So what do you think? Shall we see if we can get the Jewel Egg and help those children in the mine? Or should we just leave them to their own fate and go home?'

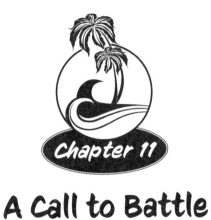

Chapter 11

A Call to Battle

Kiri's question hung in the air. Should they risk all to find the Jewel Egg and help the children in the mine? Or should they just go home? Emma said she wanted to help the children, but was scared. Jed was eager to set off straight away and find the Jewel Egg. Ethan had had enough of the island and just wanted to go home. They all spoke at once and then fell silent.

'I'm in,' said Emma after a time. She turned to her twin brother. 'What about you?'

'Okay,' said Ethan reluctantly. 'I'll go too. I can't leave you on your own.'

'Let's get going then,' said Jed, already setting out at a brisk pace. 'We don't have time to spare.' He glanced down at the shaft they had just climbed out of. 'The apes could be on to us at any time.'

'Let's go to the castle and find the giants first. We are going to need all the help we can get,' said Kiri.

'Hooray! Hooray!' chirped Wee Wig in the sky.

They began walking at a fast stride, Ethan mumbling grumpily to himself while they crossed through the lush tropical forest. However, when they reached the riverbank edge, they were in for a surprise. There in the water was a furry duck-billed creature that Kiri immediately recognised.

'Pangali!' cried Kiri, racing forward to embrace her old friend. 'What are you doing here?'

'Oh, it has been so wonderful to go home to see my family, I just wanted to come back and thank you,' said Pangali, his bill quivering with excitement.

Next to him another beak appeared and gentle brown eyes surveyed the children before disappearing below the water. Then two tiny beaks broke the surface and two younger versions of Pangali arced into the air before vanishing into the water again.

'Oh!' gasped Emma.

'That's my family,' said Pangali proudly.

Soft brown eyes peered at them again from by Pangali's side.

'Hello, Mrs Pangali,' said Kiri, before Pangali's wife hid again.

'Ah, she's a bit shy,' said Pangali while the youngsters leapt through the air again, obviously trying to outdo each other. 'Not like my children.'

'This is Emma and Ethan,' said Kiri, 'and this is Big Wig and Wee Wig Knockulous.'

Pangali was delighted to meet them and then wanted to know all the news of everything that had happened since he had swum home to his family. He was apologetic when Big Wig explained that the mine was actually *away* from Black Mountain, not *towards* it. And he was clearly shocked to hear of the plight of the children in the mine, and when he heard of their plan he offered to swim closer to the castle to act as lookout. They all agreed that was a good idea.

They set off towards the side door of the castle, Kiri fingering the key in her pocket. When they came to a stop at the bottom of the rocky ridge the castle towered above them. Emma looked at it fearfully while Kiri explained that they would have to climb up so she could let them in.

'I don't think I can do that,' Emma said eventually. 'It's so high, I think I'll fall.'

'You can do it,' said Kiri. 'Just follow me and don't look down.'

'There don't seem to be any apes around at the moment,' reported Big Wig from the air. 'I think the Chief must have them busy doing something away from the castle.'

The children climbed towards the castle wall, Big Wig and Wee Wig fluttering overhead.

'The door! The door!' cried Wee Wig excitedly as the

children edged closer.

Finally, hot and breathing heavily, Kiri was close enough to open the door. Once inside they followed Kiri through corridors and rooms of the palace until they reached the staircase to the lower level. They descended the stairs, looking at each other fearfully. When they reached the dungeon at the bottom, Kiri opened the largest of the doors. Emma let out a small shriek of alarm. Inside the room was a large slumbering giant, loudly snoring with his mouth open, dribble running down the side of his chin.

'It's all right, Emma,' said Jed. 'That's Olaf. He's the one that helped us find you.'

'That's right,' said Kiri. 'If he hadn't got us captured by the Chief's apes, we would have never been taken to the mines. It wasn't his fault though,' she added quickly, seeing Emma's alarmed look.

'The apes drugged him with something I think.

Before that he was doing a great job fighting them all off.'

'I guess ... that's all right then,' said Emma uncertainly, eyeing the large sleeping form.

'How do we wake him up?' asked Jed, walking up close to Olaf's large face. 'Wake up!' he shouted, but the giant simply continued sleeping.

'Let's trying pinching him,' said Ethan.

He grabbed some skin and pinched as hard as he could. The giant continued to peacefully snore, lost in the land of slumbers.

'Any ideas, Big Wig?' Kiri asked the brightly coloured creature hovering overhead.

'I'm very sorry, my dear child, but for this particular problem I don't know what the solution is.'

'I think we should try closing his mouth and pinching his nose,' said Jed.

'Yuck!' both the girls reacted at the same time, but Ethan simply nodded. 'Yes, that could work,' he said to Jed. 'It just might be enough to wake him if he can't breathe for a minute.'

'But you could kill him,'
wailed Emma.

'Of course we won't, Em,' said Ethan. 'We won't try this longer than a few seconds. If it doesn't work we'll stop.'

The two boys manoeuvred the giant's jaw shut, pushing under his chin until the large mouth was closed. They stood back to look at their handiwork and were pleased to see the mouth stayed put. The giant breathed the rhythmical sounds of sleep.

'Well, at least that's stopped the snoring,' said Ethan. 'Okay, who's going to pinch his nose shut?'

'Not me,' said Emma quickly. 'Ugh.'

'Not me either,' said Kiri. 'I mean, I like him for a giant, but I don't want to touch his nose.'

'Girls,' muttered Ethan and looked at Jed. 'It looks like it's a job for you and me then. I'll take one side and you can take the other.'

Using both hands they touched the bulbous nose and pushed hard.

'Yuck, his skin feels slimy,' complained Ethan. 'And look at all that snot.'

Kiri watched anxiously, trying not to think about the snot that was now leaking from one nostril like a green sludge.

Emma began to count. 'One thousand and one, one thousand and two ...'

Olaf was completely still, then there was a tremendous gurgling sound in his throat and his mouth flew open while he gasped for air, his eyes blinking awake. The boys were thrown to each side as he sat up with a start. He looked about himself with a puzzled frown, then his eyes rested on Kiri.

'Where am I?'

It was up to Kiri to explain what had happened while he extracted his handkerchief and blew his nose. It was a task that took a while. When he heard his beloved Daisy was in the cell next door he rose urgently to his feet.

'I must go to her straight away,' he declared in a loud voice.

Within two paces he was in the corridor, and without waiting for Kiri to open the neighbouring cell door he bashed in the door with the back of his hand. The door fractured like broken chopsticks before he took in the sight of Daisy in her floral frock, deeply asleep, her lips glossy with dark lipstick.

'Oh, my love!' Olaf cried and gathered her in his arms. He bent his head and kissed her fully on the lips. Jed and Ethan groaned and turned away.

'She's waking up!'
said Emma with delight.

The giantess's eyes filled with tears while she clasped her husband to her. 'Olaf, my dear. You came for me!'

'Oh Daisy! Oh course, I did.'

The children had to wait for some time as the gigantic couple kissed and embraced each other again.

'This is gross,' muttered Ethan, staring at the ceiling.

Jed was tapping his foot impatiently. 'We need to find the Jewel Egg and get out of this place. We don't have time for this.'

Emma sighed slightly and smiled. 'I think they look lovely together,' she said to Kiri. 'They're just big and cuddly. They're not scary at all.'

Big Wig and Wee Wig circled in the air, keeping an eye out for any rogue apes.

'I think I know where the Jewel Egg is,' said Kiri suddenly, and she instantly had everyone's attention. Even the kissing giants stopped to look at her, Olaf with red lipstick smeared around his mouth.

'Remember we found that room with huge steel doors that gave me an electric shock?' she asked Jed.

'Yes.'

'I think the Jewel Egg must be behind that.'

'The Jewel Egg!' cried Olaf. 'Do you really think it's here?'

'Well, the Chief lives here, so it's the most likely place, don't you think?' said Jed.

'And the room with steel doors – where is this room?' asked Olaf.

He looked set to go stomping through the palace immediately and Kiri sighed. She could picture him lumbering around breaking doors and furniture and getting lost.

There was a piercing whistle overhead and they turned to look at Big Wig flying towards them quickly. 'I hate to interrupt, but there are a large number of apes headed in this direction and the Chief is with them. We'd better move quickly.'

'How many apes, Big Wig?' asked Jed.

'Around two hundred.'

They looked at each other. Two hundred apes was a lot to deal with, even with two giants on their side. Kiri looked at the key in her hand and began to direct the group. 'Quick, let's open up all the cells. Jed and Ethan, I want you to wake the people inside this dungeon. They can help us take on the apes. I'm sure they aren't fans of the Chief so let's create our own army.'

She flung the key to Jed, who opened up the cell next to them. They began pinching the people in there awake.

'This is easier than waking giants,' Ethan muttered, pinching another person awake.

'Big Wig, fly out and let me know how much time you think we have before they arrive,' commanded Kiri.

Big Wig scuttled high into the air with Wee Wig on his tail.

'Whoosh!' cried Wee Wig.

'Daisy, would you mind looking after Emma? If you could lift her high, I'd like her to keep an eye out for any apes with arrows and she can warn us. We don't want you or Olaf being poisoned again.'

'Of course, dear,' said Daisy, and before Emma had time to say anything she was lifted high into the air, the giantess carefully cradling her like you would a little puppy. 'Oh what a cute little girl you are,' said Daisy, peering at her closely. 'You're just like a little doll. You're so pretty. Do you think I can keep you when all of this is over?'

Around them people of all shapes and sizes were appearing, rubbing their eyes like they'd been sleeping for years – which they very well might have been. Strange creatures appeared from a couple of the cells and disappeared from the castle. For a time confusion reigned and Kiri struggled to be heard over the babbling voices.

'I'd say you have about five minutes,' said Big Wig, flying

in a low arc over the throng.

'Who are all these people?' shouted Kiri.

'They're the parents that survived the violence of the Chief's actions five years ago.'

'The parents! Goodness, so some of those poor children in the mine aren't orphans after all!' cried Emma. 'That's incredible news!'

Kiri stared up at her friend for a moment, their unspoken communication giving Kiri comfort, despite the fact her parents were still dead, and always would be. Kiri then pulled a stool from one of the cells, stood on it and addressed the crowd.

'I am Kiri of the Land of the Long White Cloud,' she declared, her brown eyes shining and her dark hair rolling past her shoulders. 'The wicked Chief and his ape army have imprisoned your children and kept you in a deep sleep for many years, but today is the day you can fight to save your children. Follow me! Fight with me! And let your children be returned to you this very day.'

She jumped down from the stool and grabbed a long, thick slab of wood from the crumpled door of Daisy's cell. Jed quickly followed her lead, brandishing another slab of wood like a sword. A loud cry erupted from the group.

'Our children!' one father cried. 'Let's fight for our children.'

Olaf stepped forward and smashed several of the dungeon doors to smithereens, and the crowd rushed forward to claim their own weapons.

'Follow me!' cried Kiri, running down the corridor towards the courtyard where water flowed from the jewel-studded fountain. Already the area was filling with the apes, the Chief in the lead.

When the Chief saw the children he shrieked like a wild banshee. 'Kill those children!'

Kiri only just ducked in time to save herself when an ape hurled himself at her. Pandemonium broke out around her as parents and apes battled furiously. Jed swung his piece of wood with increasing accuracy at the apes who charged him. Ethan was shooting at the apes with his water pistol, doing a great job at holding them back since they were clearly terrified of his weapon. Whether it was the water, the laser beam or the siren, they would never know. Olaf strode through the crowd swiping five apes to the floor at a time. Daisy hung back in the doorway to the dungeon, holding Emma carefully in her hands.

'Look out!' cried Emma several times when apes tried to shoot a poisoned dart into Olaf's feet and legs. He sidestepped their attempts each time, once accidentally crushing an ape beneath him.

The Chief roared when he saw his commanding ape fall to the ground and Kiri went racing towards him, moving her slab of wood like a sword above her head. The Chief's mouth fell open and he took several steps back.

'Retreat! Retreat!' the Chief commanded, and he ran from

the courtyard, but no one but Kiri heard his command.

The parents were winning the battle, but then Olaf was suddenly felled by a poison arrow. He went crashing to the ground and very soon after began to breathe the deep slumber of a drugged sleep. The fighting around Kiri continued even more fiercely as the apes began to gain the upper hand.

Suddenly Jed was at her side, breathing heavily. 'Get out of here. Go and find the Jewel Egg.'

'But I can't let you fight this by yourself.'

'Go! You and I are the only ones who know where the room is. Big Wig and Wee Wig will go with you.'

Kiri locked eyes with Jed and could see determination written in his green eyes. She could see the sense in what he was saying. She nodded and began to run to the nearest door. Turning with a sweeping motion to see Ethan and Jed fighting back to back against hardened warrior apes, Kiri fled the room with her colourful bird-like friends close overhead. This time Wee Wig had nothing to say. He was utterly silent while he flew.

Chapter 12

The Jewel Egg

Kiri sprinted the length of the corridor and then through the opulent red, green and blue rooms of luxury, her mind focussed on the strange room with the steel doors. Confident in her step while she ran the length of each room, she instinctively remembered which way to go towards her destination. It was with calm surety that she stepped finally into the strange, empty room.

'This is it,' she said. 'I know the Jewel Egg must be behind that door.'

Big Wig landed by her feet and stared at the doors with an expression of awe. 'Yes. This is it. I can feel it.'

Kiri nodded. She now recognised an energy, a pull to whatever was behind the door, which she hadn't been aware of when she had last been in the room. Wee Wig circled overhead and suddenly yelped. There was an electric flash of blue and he plummeted to the ground.

'Oh! Wee Wig!' cried Kiri.

She peered down at the small creature. He smelt slightly singed and his eyes were closed. His wings were stuck on the colour purple.

'I say, old chap. Are you all right?' said Big Wig.

Kiri touched Wee Wig's wings gently and he stirred slightly.

'Oh,' said Wee Wig, opening his eyes and then closing them. 'Stars.' Wee Wig's wings began to slowly change colour again.

'Is he going to be all right?' Kiri asked Big Wig, who had bent down to help Wee Wig to his wobbly feet.

'Yes, he'll be fine. He's very resilient, our Wee Wig,' said Big Wig, affectionately ruffling his red scorched mop. 'Even if he is a silly goose sometimes.'

Wee Wig opened his eyes again and smiled at them goofily. 'Oh! Stars! Lots of stars,' he said happily.

'See,' said Big Wig. 'Nothing ever gets him down. He's got a splendid disposition.'

Wee Wig did seem to be okay, although he wobbled around the room for a few moments muttering about stars. When Big Wig and Kiri were confident he was truly all right they turned their attention again to the problem of how to open the steel doors.

'Any thoughts of how we turn off the electric field?' mused Kiri.

'There must be a switch or button somewhere.'

They looked carefully around the room. The walls and ceiling were perfectly plain; there wasn't a hint of a button anywhere. Kiri began feeling the walls up and down, methodically working around the room. She couldn't feel anything. Frustrated, she was pacing the room impatiently when she noticed that a section of the floor felt uneven under her feet. She paused for a moment and then dropped to her knees.

'Oh! I think I've found something!' she said, looking closely at the floor.

What she could now see was a small square, barely perceptible in the middle of the room. She touched the square gently and a lid immediately sprang up under her touch. Under the lid was a jewel-topped button, which she pushed without hesitation.

There was a whirring noise and the steel doors slowly opened. Kiri rose to her feet, and with Big Wig in the air, and Wee Wig wobbling in circles on the ground, they inched forward. The steel doors opened to reveal a strange new room, infused with sparking light. On a stand in the centre of the room was a large egg-shaped jewel which shone with all the colours of the rainbow.

'Oh, how beautiful,' said Kiri, standing close to the strange jewel, her face awash with rays of different colours.

'That's it,' said Big Wig. 'That's the Jewel Egg.'

'Pretty,' said Wee Wig.

Kiri's attention turned to the rest of the room. It was the oddest thing. In one corner of the room was a shimmering pile of pebbles. In the other corner was a large pile of shells. They were just like the pebbles and shells they had found on the beach when they had first arrived.

'This is very strange,' she murmured. 'Why are all these pebbles and shells in this room with the Jewel Egg?'

'They must be important,' said Big Wig.

'I think I'll take a couple with us. You're right, they must be important to be locked away like this.'

Kiri walked forward and picked up two perfectly round pebbles. They too shone with different colours. She put the two pebbles in her pocket. She selected two shells that looked like they could have been a pair and put them in her pocket also.

'We should go,' said Big Wig, sounding anxious.

'You're right,' said Kiri.

She carefully removed the Jewel Egg from the stand, and she could feel the strange jewel pulsing beneath her fingertips.

'It's a shame I don't have anything to put this in,' she said, tucking it under her arm.

'Your friend has a bag,' said Big Wig.

'You mean Ethan? He's a knucklehead, not a friend, but you are right, he does have a bag. That could be very useful.'

Kiri set off at a slow gait, finding it hard to run with a giant jewel under her arm. The Jewel Egg illuminated the corridors and rooms they passed through with light of every colour. Wee Wig couldn't fly again yet and was having problems walking, so after a short discussion Big Wig convinced him to climb on his back, and now Big Wig flew near Kiri's head, puffing slightly with the extra weight.

When they entered the courtyard the battle was still in fierce progress and the apes appeared to be winning. Olaf and Daisy were both flat on their backs snoring loudly, and scattered around the room parents were crumpled on the ground like discarded dolls.

Jed was fighting manfully, one to one with an ape. He saw Kiri just after he managed a blow with his wood stick that sent the ape flying to the floor.

'You've got it!' he cried. 'We'd better get out of here.'

'Where are the twins?' asked Kiri.

Ethan was battling with another ape, hand to hand. It seemed his water pistol was no longer working. Jed ran over to help him.

'Emma! Where are you?' Kiri shouted.

A small voice came from the inside of Daisy's hand. 'I'm in here,' cried Emma. 'But I can't get out.'

'Are you hurt?' Kiri rushed forward.

'I'm fine. I just can't push Daisy's fingers open.'

Kiri put the Jewel Egg on the ground and tackled the large fingers, one by one, pulling with all of her weight until they slowly spread open. Emma climbed out gingerly as the boys appeared at their sides.

'I need your backpack,' said Kiri to Ethan.

'Well, you can't have it, it's mine.'

'I need it to carry this, you idiot,' she said, taking the Jewel Egg from beside Daisy. It sparkled and shone as she lifted it up.

'WOW!' said Jed.
'Fantastic!' said Ethan.
'Oh,' said Emma.

For a moment the Jewel Egg sent dazzling rainbow lights all around the room. Mesmerised, Ethan silently handed Kiri the backpack.

'Do you mind if I take care of the bag from now on?' Kiri asked Ethan, placing the Jewel Egg in the bag.

'You take it,' said Ethan abruptly – and Kiri had the distinct feeling he didn't want the responsibility of guarding it.

There was a shriek and a roar when the Chief burst into the courtyard.

'The invaders from the Land of the Long White Cloud

have stolen the Jewel Egg!' he thundered, his face purple. 'After them!'

But his words seemed to revitalise the few parents that were still standing. They formed a ragged line and charged at the apes that were surging forward to obey the Chief's orders.

'Let's get out of here!' shouted Jed, and the children set off at fast pace.

They tore past the slumbering Daisy, and through the dungeon and up the stairs of the palace. They exited through the side gate, clambering down the rocky hill.

'Head for the forest,' shouted Big Wig from above. 'You need to take the Jewel Egg back past Black Mountain and then on to Free Bay. Only Princess Makana will know what you need to do next. But hurry, the apes are just behind you.'

Kiri looked behind them nervously to see that the apes were pouring from the castle gates. The sight of them urged her to pick up her pace. They plunged into the forest, Jed and Kiri leading the way through the tropical bush. On and on they ran, with the sounds of the apes seeming to get closer and closer.

'Don't forget the cave!' shouted a voice – and Kiri recognised the flourish that Pangali made when he hit the water. The cave! Of course.

'Follow me,' she cried, and within minutes the children were crushed into the small dark space that she and Jed had previously hid in.

'Ow!' complained Ethan to Emma. 'You're standing on my foot.'

'Shhh,' whispered Jed, looking upwards. 'They're coming this way now.'

And so the apes were. With wild cries in the air, the ground began to shudder. Then they heard the deep tones of the Chief. 'Find those children. I don't care if they are dead or alive – just get me back my Jewel Egg.'

Kiri noticed that Emma had closed her eyes, covered her hands over her ears and was biting her lip. Ethan became paler than he was naturally. Jed and Kiri glanced at each other and then stared silently upward, their every sense alert and listening. The roars and grunts of the apes finally began to fade away, and then there was nothing but the sound of birds and the water flowing in the river. The children remained where they were for a few more moments, their hearts pounding. It was only then that Kiri realised how close she was to Jed, and blushing she stepped away from him.

'You're safe to come out now,' said a quiet voice above them. It was Big Wig, whispering.

'Safe, safe,' chirped Wee Wig.

The children clambered out into the mid-afternoon air. Pangali waved at them from the river.

'I think you will be safest if you follow the river past Black Mountain,' he said. 'I know a few other hiding spots if things get sticky.'

So began a frantic chase of cat and mouse as the children,

Big Wig and Wee Wig, and Pangali made their way towards
Black Mountain. Every so often the children scurried for
safety while the apes moved back and forth searching for
them, shrieking for their blood. It seemed the Chief was
somehow drawn to the power of the Jewel Egg and every
time they thought the apes had gone for good, they would
hear the Chief roaring, 'No, go that way, fools. Over there!'

The hours wore on, and it became darker and darker as
they entered the base of Black Mountain – and they became
more tired, hungry and scared. Only Kiri seemed to draw on
some inner strength from somewhere and she urged them to
carry on. On and on they walked, Emma's feet now covered
in blisters. Ethan began muttering about how dark it was
and that he couldn't see. Jed's stomach howled with hunger.

Overhead Big Wig and Wee Wig acted as scouts for
whenever the apes got too close. From the river Pangali
directed them to the hideouts he knew of. They were
squashed into another small hole when Emma began to cry.

'Hey, hey,' said Ethan, hesitating for a moment, and then
putting his arm around his sister. 'It's okay. We're almost
there, I think.'

'But it's so dark and I'm so hungry,' sobbed Emma. 'And I
don't like the apes. What if they capture us and kill us?'

'They won't do that,' said Kiri fiercely. 'I won't let them.'

Emma hiccupped and began to look slightly calmer.

'It'll be okay,' said Jed. 'I'm sure we'll be past Black
Mountain soon. And once we get to Free Bay we'll be safe.

Then we'll be able to go home.'

'Home!' Emma brightened at the thought. 'You know, I miss home.'

'I know,' said Ethan, patting her on the back.

Big Wig's voice appeared out of the gloom. 'I think we can press on, children. The apes seem to have disappeared.'

The children clambered out of the hole and they marched onwards, sparse conversation now almost too hard for them because they were exhausted.

'Do you think we should use the Jewel Egg for light?'
said Emma, stumbling over an exposed root of a dead plant in the dark.

'I don't know. What about the apes?' said Kiri. 'We don't want to draw them to us.'

Emma sighed.

'I'm sure we're almost there,' said Jed. 'Look, there's a little bit of light up ahead.'

Emma peered into the distance. 'Perhaps,' she said doubtfully.

'Just think how far we've come,' said Ethan in a falsely bright voice. 'We survived being captured by the Chief, we escaped the mine, and we even fought the apes and captured the Jewel Egg. I think that's pretty impressive, all in all! I'm sure nothing can go wrong now.'

Kiri knew Ethan was trying to cheer his sister up, but they were to discover he had never been more wrong in his life. A far-off swooping noise was the first sign of trouble. The second was Big Wig's frantic cry for the children to take cover. It wasn't the apes this time. It was something much more sinister.

Chapter 13

The Deadly Attacking Bats

Big Wig's warning rang in the air and the sky filled with a swarm of dark, menacing creatures. They had enormous black wings and eyes the colour of blood.

'Bats!' screamed Emma.

The children scrambled for cover. Three or four of the dark beasts lunged at Emma, attacking her with their razor-sharp claws. She crumpled to the ground, blood pouring from gashed open wounds.

'Emma!' cried Ethan.

He grabbed a large stick and began beating the bats away. He had never seen anything more evil in his life, these black, sinister creatures, screeching and circling like vultures. Jed and Kiri rushed to help him, plucking rocks from the ground and hurling them at the vicious bats, who continued to attack a senseless Emma.

The bats swirled and swooped in the air, now trying to claw Jed, Kiri and Ethan, their cries bloodcurdling and wild. One of them savagely tried to slash Kiri, but they missed her arm and instead the creature ripped the backpack from her shoulder. The bag hit the ground and fell open, and a dazzling sparkle of colourful light suddenly splintered the darkness. The bats screamed with horror, frantically circling away from the light, banging into each other in their desperation to get away.

Kiri stood slowly, raising the luminous jewel in her hand, its light shattering the darkness so it was a rainbow of jewelled colours. The bats were clearly terrified of the light and sped as fast as they could to get away from it. Soon the children could no longer hear their cries. Kiri turned to face her friends. Jed and Ethan were leaning over Emma and were in muttered conversation. That's when Kiri noticed the blood seeping from Emma's arms and legs. Even her face had a claw mark running down it.

'Oh, Em!' she cried, racing forward and kneeling by her best friend. 'She's not–'

'She's alive,' said Jed quickly. 'She's breathing.'

'But look at all the blood! If we don't get some help she could, she could–' She couldn't say her worst fear out loud.

'We need to get to Free Bay as soon as we can, but in the meantime we need to do something to stop this bleeding.'

Jed began to peel off his t-shirt and Kiri hastily looked away. 'We need to cut this into strips.'

He pulled his Swiss army knife from his pocket and began cutting up his t-shirt. Kiri put the Jewel Egg carefully on top of the backpack and used each strip of fabric to wrap the worst of the wounds on her friend's arms and legs.

Pangali shouted from the river, 'Is Emma okay?'

'She's very hurt,' said Kiri.
'Is it much further to Free Bay?'

'Not far,' said Pangali. 'In about a mile we leave Black Mountain. After that we'll be in Free Bay. It will take us a while to get to the township, but it will be light then and the path will be easy.'

'How are we going to carry Emma?' said Ethan, looking around. 'We need to make a stretcher out of something.'

'Around the next corner of the river is a large plant – you'll be able to use one of the leaves,' said Big Wig, circling above. 'They look strong enough.'

Ethan broke into a run and disappeared around the corner. After a few moments he emerged with an enormous leaf in his arms. It was a reddy brown colour and when the children examined it, it felt thick and sturdy, but still soft and supple. Ethan placed the large leaf on the ground next to his sister and then the boys carefully lifted her on to it. Emma moaned slightly, but didn't open her eyes. She looked pale and fragile lying on the large leaf, dressed in her tatty long party dress, her arms and legs bound with strips of Jed's t-shirt. Ethan and Jed took hold of an end of the leaf each and began walking. Kiri led the way, holding the Jewel Egg in her hands both for light and to keep the bats away. If only she had used the Jewel Egg for light when Emma had suggested it, her friend would never have been hurt. The knowledge pained Kiri to her core.

'The apes are a couple of miles back,' reported Big Wig. 'But don't worry, they won't go into Free Bay. When we leave Black Mountain we'll be safe.'

'Why won't they follow us?'
asked Jed.

'The Chief is terrified of his sister. He'd never send the apes after us there.'

'Princess Makana is Chief Namba's sister?' said Kiri. 'But who's to say she's any better than him?'

'Oh, don't worry,' said Pangali, splashing in the river, 'Princess Makana is the kindest, wisest ruler that Trinity Island has ever had. She'll put everything right.'

When the children walked further they could see sunlight on the horizon, the sun breaking into the sky.

'Goodness!' said Kiri. 'It must be morning. We've been walking all afternoon and night past Black Mountain. It's been so dark, I've completely lost track of time.'

She put the Jewel Egg carefully into Ethan's backpack. They didn't need it for light or safety now.

'I haven't lost track of time,' Ethan mumbled.

'I wonder how many meals we've missed in that time,' said Jed.

Tired and hungry, the children walked on in silence. The path they followed by the riverbank became wider, and when the sun rose in the sky they noticed that the landscape had changed. It was tropical and lush, but seemed more manicured than Jewel Lagoon. There seemed to be an order to everything around them. Pangali shouted encouragement from the river while they trudged along.

There was a flurry in the air and a group of knockulouses suddenly appeared in the sky.

'Big Wig! Wee Wig!' said one of their brightly coloured group. 'Old chaps! We haven't seen you for ages. What have you been doing?'

Like Big Wig and Wee Wig, they all had bright red hair, wings that changed colour and different-coloured bow ties.

'The Jewel Egg! The Jewel Egg!' squeaked Wee Wig before Big Wig could give them a sensible answer.

The group of knockulouses stared at the four children struggling along the road, and there was a long, excited conversation in the sky about the Chief and his apes, the Jewel Egg and their escape. The knockulouses seemed to be talking all at once, so the children couldn't make out much of the conversation. Then, without warning, the group of knockulouses flew off, clearly in a hurry.

'Where are they going?' asked Kiri. 'They didn't even say goodbye.'

'Sorry about that, my dear. They were a bit excited. It's not every day you see a country's destiny being fulfilled,' said Big Wig. 'They are sending word to the Princess that you're on your way.'

Indeed, it seemed that the knockulouses had done their work quickly when only moments later a white horse and carriage appeared travelling down the road towards them. It came to a stop in front of the children. A kindly-looking man with bushy eyebrows peered down at them.

'Welcome to Free Bay, dear children,' he said in a rich baritone voice.

He leapt from the driver's seat and opened the door for them. 'Her Majesty requests your presence.'

The man bent down and lifted Emma into his arms. 'The poor child is burning up,' he said when Emma rolled against him. She moaned quietly and seemed to stir. 'We'd best get you to the Princess quickly.' He placed her carefully on one of the seats in the carriage.

Pangali waved at them from the river. 'Good luck, children!' he said. 'Off you go!'

'Bye bye,' chirped Wee Wig in the air.

'The Princess will tell you what you need to do,' said Big Wig. 'Don't worry, everything will be fine now.'

'Thank you for everything,' said Kiri, waving to each of them.

The boys looked at each other, clambered in and sat together on one of the seats. Kiri sat on the other seat with her friend, lifting Emma's head on to her lap.

'Do help yourself to something to eat and drink,' said the driver before shutting the door. 'Although it won't be long and we'll be at the palace.'

The carriage began to move forward at a steady pace and the children looked around them. The inside of the carriage was light and airy. The seats were a simple creamy colour and the carriage walls were adorned with a delicate gold leaf pattern against the pale background. The boys couldn't see any food and looked at each other with puzzled expressions.

'How can we help ourselves to something to eat if there isn't anything here?' mumbled Ethan. 'I'm so hungry! What kind of bad joke is this?'

He fidgeted in his seat and then noticed a small gold button on the wall. He pushed it distractedly. There was a whirring sound and a table began to rise between the opposing seats from the floor. On it was laid the most wonderful food and drink the children had ever seen.

There were hot chips, roasted chicken, small savoury pies, corn on the cob dripping with lashings of butter, and the desserts – they looked simply scrumptious. Chocolate mud cake with gooey rich chocolate sauce, ice cream sundaes with delicious smooth strawberry sauce and cream-filled chocolate éclairs were all waiting to be eaten. Everything was presented on beautiful white and gold platters. Jed and Ethan didn't hesitate to load their plates as high as they could go.

Kiri felt Emma's forehead and looked down at her with worry. Emma *was* burning up, and that couldn't be good. Emma stirred and muttered in her sleep, but Kiri couldn't make out what she was saying. Kiri glanced out the window for a moment, noticing the beauty of Free Bay as they passed by. Everywhere Kiri looked she saw smiling people and children, neatly dressed in light-coloured, flowing clothing. There were little bamboo cottages with large verandas set against the backdrop of the tropical beauty, the plants and foliage all perfectly kept and maintained. The river disappeared out of view and then they were passing long white sand beaches, with children frolicking in the waves, laughing and joking. It was a paradise, there was no doubt. The carriage continued and the road became busier as other carriages jostled around them. There were also more houses. It seemed they were nearing the township.

'Have something to eat,' said Jed, with his mouth half full. 'This food is fantastic.'

Kiri felt beyond hunger, the worry for her friend the only thing paining her stomach now, but she realised she hadn't eaten for a long time so she selected a piece of chicken and some hot chips and nibbled on those.

'Look at this!' said Ethan, gazing out the window, his mouth open in astonishment.

They had just passed through curling white gates that swung open at their approach. The carriage slowed and they went down a long driveway that had beautiful white rose gardens and elegant fountains on each side. Then they curved off around a large statue of an athletic woman with long flowing hair riding a horse. The statue was in the middle of the circular driveway and they came to rest at the entrance of a huge, glittering white and gold palace. Two young men dressed in white and gold embroidered jackets walked forward and opened their door with a bow.

'Welcome, o ye of the Land of the Long White Cloud,'
announced one of them in a formal voice.

'Er, thanks,' said Ethan, getting out first. 'Jolly good.'

'One of the girls is injured,' said the driver, getting down from his post.

Immediately one of the young men disappeared only to reappear with two men dressed in long white cloaks. Jed and Kiri climbed out of the carriage, while one of the men disappeared into the carriage to look at Emma. He whispered to his colleague and they gently lifted her out of the carriage and laid her on a stretcher. They began to walk away.

'Where are they taking her?' asked Kiri.

'Don't worry,' said one of the men in the embroidered jackets. 'She'll be in the care of the best doctors in the land. They are taking her to the palace hospital. You'll be able to visit her soon. In the meantime, please follow me.'

There seemed nothing to do but obey, so the children fell into line behind the two men, who led them down a long, light hallway to two large doors. Kiri couldn't help comparing it with the Chief's castle, which had been darkly and richly opulent, but cold and impersonal. This palace was light and simple, and it radiated a warmth and happiness that made her feel good.

'The children from the Land of the Long White Cloud,' announced an official in a loud voice while the men swung the two doors open wide.

The children stepped into a large room, glittering in white and gold, while people dressed in long flowing clothes milled around. At the end of the room was a large throne. The children edged towards the throne along the fine gold-coloured carpet. The people in the room became quiet while they watched the children stand before the Princess.

Instinctively, Kiri curtsied awkwardly and the boys tried to bow low.

'Dear children,' said the voice from the throne. 'I am Princess Makana, the ruler of Free Bay. It is so good of you to be here. Please rise and come closer.'

The Princess's voice was warm, firm and inviting. It was the voice of a young woman, but when the children rose they found themselves looking into the dull blue eyes of a withered old crone, bent over as though she had bad arthritis. Her hands visibly shook, and her legs were twisted beneath her like dead twigs. She wore a flowing white dress with gold edging at its neckline and hem, and a gold crown on her stooped white-haired head.

'What are your names?' inquired the Princess in a kind voice.

'I'm Jed, your Majesty.' Jed sounded shy.

'I'm Ethan, your Highness,' Ethan mumbled.

'I am Kiri from the Land of the Long White Cloud,' said Kiri in a clear but respectful voice. There was a murmur from the crowd behind her.

'Kiri,' murmured the Princess. 'What happened to your friend, Emma? My personal physician said she was badly injured.'

'Bats attacked us when we were travelling through Black Mountain,' said Kiri.

At the mention of bats and Black Mountain the crowd in the room collectively gasped. A courtier approached the Princess and whispered in her ear.

'Emma will soon be restored to full health,' said the Princess. 'Our doctors say she is now resting comfortably. You will be able to see her again soon.'

'Thank you, your Majesty,' said Kiri.

'I think you have something for me,' said the Princess with a gentle smile.

Kiri remembered the Jewel Egg in her bag and bent to take it out.

'Yes, I do,' she said.

Kiri lifted the Jewel Egg with both hands, holding it upwards to the Princess. The room shone with the radiance of a brilliant rainbow and filled with shimmering jewel colours. The crowd gasped again, this time in wonder.

The Princess's voice filled the room. 'Today, my kin people, is the beginning of the end of tyranny in our lands. It is the end of betrayal and deceit. Today is the beginning of a united Trinity Island once more, where all wrongs will be righted.'

The Princess's courtiers stepped forward to take the Jewel Egg from Kiri. They put it carefully on a stand by the Princess's throne. The Princess smiled at Kiri, Jed and Ethan, her blue eyes resting on them each in turn.

'Tonight we will hold a feast in your honour and then you must rest. Tomorrow we will journey to Black Mountain and we will restore the Jewel Egg to its rightful place.'

Chapter 14

The Jewel Egg is Restored

That evening at Princess Makana's palace would live on in Kiri's mind forever. The children were taken to see Emma, who was lying in bed, awake and smiling. They didn't know what the doctors had done to her, but she looked healthy and normal, without even the hint of a scratch. The doctors wanted to keep her in for observation, but said tomorrow she would be fit to join the group to journey to Black Mountain.

'Have you told Princess Makana about the children in the mines?' Emma asked.

The children explained that the Princess knew all about them, but no one had been able to travel successfully through Black Mountain to help them. All the rescue parties they had sent had been lost forever – so in the end the Princess had to ban people from going near Black Mountain. It was deemed to be too dangerous.

'So how did we make it through then?' asked Emma.

Big Wig and Wee Wig were circling the children in the air. 'Bravery and resilience,' said Big Wig.

'Brave! Brave!' Wee Wig shrilled, and then hiccupped.

'I think it was just a bit of luck,' said Kiri modestly. 'And we had the Jewel Egg with us, didn't we? The Princess said that gives good people protection from evil.'

Then she thought of Jed being attacked by the giant centipede on their first trip to Black Mountain and had to suppress a shudder. It was a shame they hadn't had the Jewel Egg then.

The three children chatted with Emma for a bit, but then she began to look sleepy so courtiers took them to their rooms, which were light and airy with adjoining bathrooms. There they washed and changed into new clothes that were ready waiting for them. They were brand new versions of the clothes they had been wearing when the carriage had picked them up. Kiri and Jed were in shorts and t-shirts, and Ethan in his nice trousers and shirt that the Chief had made him wear on the night they first arrived on the island.

'I wonder how they made us new clothes so quickly?' said Kiri to Jed when they were being escorted to the feasting hall. She looked at his new t-shirt. Of course, the previous one they had ripped up to help Emma.

'I've been wondering that myself,' said Jed. 'Especially since no one here dresses like we do.' They looked about them again. Everyone was dressed in long, flowing cream clothing. 'What do you think, Ethan?'

But for once Ethan didn't have a theory to offer.

When they arrived at the feasting hall they were led to three seating places by the Princess. Kiri sat on one side of her, Jed and Ethan sat on the other. The children looked out across a vast table, people smiling cheerfully at them. The Princess commanded everyone to charge their glasses. Goblets with foaming, creamy drinks were put into the children's hands.

'I invite you to drink to our guests.' She turned to Kiri in her seat and gave her a nod. 'Kiri from the Land of the Long White Cloud.' The crowd roared their approval and then the Princess turned to Jed. 'Jed from the Land of the Long White Cloud.' Again the crowd clapped and cheered before the Princess turned to Ethan. 'Ethan from the Land of the Long White Cloud.' The Princess faced the group. 'And to Emma, from the Land of the Long White Cloud, who can't be with us in person tonight, but who is with us in spirit. Let us drink to their courage and bravery in bringing us the Jewel Egg. To the children from the Land of the Long White Cloud!' The people in the room raised their glasses towards the children and then drank from them.

Kiri felt herself go red with all the attention, but once she had sipped her creamy drink and discovered how delicious it was she felt calmer. The liquid seemed to spread a warm glow through her body. The evening progressed and there was wonderful food and entertainment. Musicians with string instruments came out and played for them. The tables were cleared and then there was singing and dancing.

'Sing for us!' cried someone from the crowd, gesturing at the children.

'Crikey,' said Jed, looking at Ethan, who was staring at his shoes. 'I don't want to sing. I can't sing in tune.'

'I'll sing,' said Kiri, after a pause. She stepped up on to the stage and looked at the musicians. 'Um, you might not know this song.'

'Don't worry,' one of them said. 'We'll follow your lead. I'm sure we'll pick it up.'

So Kiri turned to face the crowd and began to sing the first verse of one of her favourite songs – one that was special to her because her mother used to sing it to her before she died.

Amazing grace, how sweet the sound
That saved a wretch like me
I once was lost but now am found
Was blind but now I see

When Kiri began to sing the second verse the band had joined in. When she had finished the third verse there was barely a dry eye in the house.

'That was beautiful, my dear,' said the Princess. 'Simply beautiful.'

'Girl, you can seriously sing,' said Jed.

'Not bad,' admitted Ethan.

Much later the children retired sleepily to their rooms, and Kiri was instantly asleep when her head hit the pillow. She dreamt of home while she slept peacefully in her comfortable bed. She woke in the morning to gentle sunlight, and when she saw the others each of them declared afterwards it was the best night's rest they had ever had. After breakfast they were reunited with a bright-eyed Emma (who looked very pretty in her long sparkling blue dress) and led to one of two waiting carriages. One was for them, and Kiri shivered with delight when she realised the Princess would be travelling with them. The other carriage was for the Princess's women, who were going to accompany them.

'We will travel to the edge of the Black Mountain,'
said the Princess, sitting amongst them, wearing a long white coat.

'From there we will walk to the sacred site and restore the Jewel Egg to its rightful place.'

'But how will you walk?' asked Ethan, looking at the Princess's crippled legs. Kiri nudged him in the ribs at the tactlessness of his question.

'I'll manage with some help,' the Princess said with a smile, although her body was stooped and shaking slightly.

So they set out in their carriages until they reached the edge of the darkness that signified Black Mountain. The Princess shuffled from the carriage and the children followed her, each of them worried about how she was going to make it up the mountain. The Princess's women alighted from their carriage. They were beautiful women: tall, athletic and strong. They were dressed in short white dresses that left one bronzed shoulder bare. Each of them had a bow and arrows slung over their back, and a sword on their hips. Kiri noticed that the boys were staring at the women. She raised her eyebrows at Ethan and he blushed when she caught his eye.

The Princess turned to Kiri.
'Would you walk with me?' she asked her.

'Of course, your Majesty,' she said, standing by the Princess.

'And Jed, will you walk with me on the other side?'

'Yes, your Highness.' Jed moved to the opposite side, and the Princess placed an arm around the shoulder of each of them.

'Ethan, will you walk in front of us and hold the Jewel Egg?'

Ethan, who had looked miffed at not being asked to help

the Princess, brightened immediately, adjusting the straps on his backpack. 'Yes, your Majesty!'

'Emma, please walk alongside him.' Emma quickly stepped to take her place, looking very happy to be walking beside her brother.

Ethan took the Jewel Egg reverently from one of the Princess's women and held it up, carefully walking in front of the Princess, but following the Princess's women, who confidently set out even though none of them knew the path before them. So they all began to walk up the mountain, the Princess supported by two of the children from the Land of the Long White Cloud. It was a long slow journey, especially because the Princess was so feeble and unsteady on her feet. As they slowly climbed the Princess uttered the occasional word of encouragement to the group, her voice melodious and strong, and more than once the children wondered how she could sound so young, but be so old and infirm in body.

With the Jewel Egg held by Ethan they could see their path clearly and it was obvious no creature dared come near them. Occasionally there was the shadow of movement far off in the distance, and Kiri thought of the giant centipedes, the apes and the bats, but then she looked at the beautiful rainbow-coloured light of the Jewel Egg and she relaxed.

When they reached Olaf's house, the Princess's women announced that they thought they were nearly there – and indeed they were right. A hundred paces or so and the group reached a large flat clearing right at the top of the ridge of

Black Mountain. On this clearing was a generous smooth rock that was as wide as a house. On top of this rock was a pole with an empty holder at its top. It was clearly the Jewel Egg's resting place. Instinctively the group formed a circle around the pole. They waited for Princess Makana's instruction.

'Ethan, please hand me the Jewel Egg,' said the Princess.

The children stepped back respectfully while Ethan handed the Princess the egg with a small bow. Everyone watched as the Princess struggled forward, moving with slow unstable steps towards the pole. At one stage the Princess seemed almost to stumble and fall, but then she righted herself and continued. Then she was at the base of the pole and for a moment she paused and caught her breath. Then she shouted into the sky, in a clear strong voice that could've been heard for miles.

'I am Princess Makana, ruler of Free Bay, Black Mountain and Jewel Lagoon. I am the ruler of Trinity Island and it is with this authority that I restore the Jewel Egg to its rightful place. May peace and harmony prevail in our lands once again.'

They watched while she carefully lifted the Jewel Egg on to its holder. Then there was a blinding flash, and a roar, and the earth trembled beneath them so violently that the children were thrown to the ground. The entire mountain seemed to rumble and far away there was the sound of shrieks and screaming. Then all was completely still.

Kiri was the first to open her eyes. The Jewel Egg was shining brightly from its stand, more beautiful than she had ever seen it, the light and colour it was producing rich and strong. She realised the colours it had shone before were but a pale imitation of its real power and beauty. She turned and around them there was clear sunlight and the mountain that had previously been plunged into darkness was now bathed in bright light. And the mountain was changing. They were at the highest point and she could see plants and grass sprouting up from the valley at an astonishing rate. Within a few moments the mountain was no longer sparse and rocky and empty of living plants, but instead bursting to life with the most wonderful greenery she had ever seen. Colourful birds sang from freshly sprung trees. The other children were getting to their feet also and gazed around with wide-eyed wonder.

Kiri looked back towards the Jewel Egg and suddenly noticed the regal form of Princess Makana. Her head was bowed, her body stooped but perfectly still, and a ripple of colour from the Jewel Egg was pulsating up and down her body.

'Look,' said Emma in a small voice, next to Kiri. 'The Princess is changing!'

They watched in astonishment while the Princess slowly began to grow taller. As she grew, she lifted herself up, no longer stooping. She threw off her long coat, and turned and lifted an arm and watched while the wrinkled white flesh became smooth and bronzed. Under her coat she was wearing a short dress in the same style as her women, but instead of white it looked like pure gold. Kiri watched as her figure changed from hunched and misshapen to a young woman with a strong, athletic figure. The Princess lifted her head high, her short white hair rapidly becoming long and golden. For a moment she closed her eyes and breathed in deeply, like she was infused with new energy. Then she opened her eyes, took a step forward and turned and swept the group with her blazing blue eyes.

'I am myself again,'
the Princess said.

Even before Princess Makana's women had bowed low, the children instinctively dropped to their knees at the sight of her.

'Rise, dear children,' the Princess said quickly.

'But, but–' Ethan stammered, but he was the first to rise to his feet.

'Yes, I know. I am young again,' said the Princess, striding with energy and confidence along the large stone, using it as a stage. 'By restoring the Jewel Egg I have broken the dark curse that Namba placed on me and I am myself again, rather than being imprisoned in a feeble old body.'

'You mean the Chief, your brother, placed this curse on you?' asked Ethan.

'Namba is no Chief, and he is not my brother although I hear he spread that rumour far and wide,' said the Princess. 'Namba is from another land, far, far away. He was a Parking Meter Warden in his country, although I don't know what that position entails. He came here more than six years ago and we gave him our hospitality but then one day we woke up to find that he had gone. Using information he had gathered from our books and studies he had quietly been raising up an army of apes, and he stole the Jewel Egg for its power.'

The Princess paused. 'He thought he would be ruler of Trinity Island, and that I would give in because I was trapped in an old body, but he underestimated my will and the will of my people. That was a terrible time. He murdered Queen Namele, my mother, and Black Mountain was plunged into darkness and all manner of evil creatures inhabited this place. Fierce battles raged between my people and his apes – but we prevailed and drove him from Free Bay.'

The Princess stood and turned her back on the children and gazed towards Jewel Lagoon. 'But now dear children, it is time to go to Jewel Lagoon. It is time to right all the wrongs Namba has inflicted on our land. It is time to liberate all of our children stuck in his terrible mine.'

She turned and looked at the children with passion and conviction shining in her eyes. 'Let us be off right away.'

Chapter 15

Freedom at Last!

The Princess, her attendants and the children walked briskly down the mountain. The journey was vastly different from their trip up. There was light, birds sang and lush, tropical plants swayed in the warm breeze. Everything around them buzzed with life, although occasionally the children caught a brief glimpse of the carcass of a dead centipede or bat, but that only made them feel even happier. They were going to Jewel Lagoon. They were going to help rescue the children in the mines. And then they were going to go home. Kiri knew that Emma, most especially, was looking forward to that.

While they tramped down the mountain the children were filled with questions, and because the Princess was in such a buoyant mood, they didn't even think to feel shy about asking her anything that came into their heads.

'Your Majesty,' said Kiri. 'Weren't you worried when you knew we were from the Land of the Long White Cloud which sounds similar to Namba's world?'

'No, not at all. Just because people come from the same place, doesn't mean that they are all going to act in the same manner. Everyone takes individual responsibility for the way they choose to behave – or at least they should.'

'Your Majesty.' Ethan was quick to jump in with the next question. 'Why is this called Black Mountain? I thought it was because it was dark, but–'

'But it isn't, is it!' finished the Princess. 'This isn't called Black Mountain because it is dark, or evil, or anything like that. Let me show you why we call this Black Mountain. Reach down and grab up a handful of soil.'

Ethan quickly did as instructed. The soil was darker than chocolate brown; it was a brown so dark it was almost black.

'That's why,' said the Princess. 'The soil is black, rich and full of nutrients. That's why this mountain is called Black Mountain. It has the richest soil in the country, and it grows the most beautiful of all the plants on Trinity Island.'

The Princess noticed that Emma was looking worried. 'What is troubling you, my dear?' she inquired.

'It's just … it's only … how are we going to beat the Chief – I mean, Namba – and the apes? There are only a few of us, and many of them.'

The Princess smiled. 'Namba won't be a problem. Now he doesn't have the Jewel Egg, he doesn't have much power. As for the apes, my women and I will deal with them.'

The Princess opened her coat slightly and it was then that Kiri noticed the long slim sword, encased in a white and gold sheath.

'But you only have girls with you,' said Ethan, and then turned red when the Princess turned to stare at him.

'My women are warriors,'
said the Princess evenly, after a moment.
'Trust me, they are a formidable force.'

Then she turned and looked at all the children in turn. 'But dear children, you have been through so much, perhaps it is a question of trust. Perhaps you feel uncomfortable about going on this mission with us. Perhaps you would like to go home right now. You can leave now if you want to.'

'No,' said Kiri. 'It is important that we help free the children before we go home.'

'I want to go home right now, but I couldn't go home knowing they were still down in the mines,' said Emma. She shivered. 'It's a terrible place.'

'We have a job to do,' said Jed simply.

'And you, Ethan?' inquired the Princess.

'I'm not going to leave Emma behind,' said Ethan. 'And it

does seem the right thing to do, helping the children down there. Em's right, it's a really rotten place.'

At the edge of Black Mountain the Princess insisted they all stop and rest. Her women produced small delicious raspberry-flavoured biscuits for everyone to eat. The Princess faced the group when they had finished eating.

'It is now time to reclaim the palace at Jewel Lagoon,' she said in a clear, firm voice. 'Children, I don't want you to be in any danger, so it is best that you are armed. Bring them their swords,' she commanded.

One of her women quickly moved forward and gave each of the children an individual sword in a sheath. Jed had the largest, then Kiri and Ethan. Emma's was the smallest, but she whispered to Kiri that she especially liked the diamonds on its handle.

'These swords are purely a precaution. You will be under the protection of my women when we move into enemy territory.' She looked at Ethan, who blushed again under her searching stare.

'To the castle!' cried the Princess, and her women moved so quickly the children had to run to keep up. They covered now familiar ground until they were walking up the road that led to the castle. The Princess looked around her.

'This is a disgrace!' she fumed. 'Where are the people? The houses? The throngs?'

It was then that there was a mighty roar and shriek and a group of around thirty apes appeared from behind the rocks. The Princess's women sent a flurry of arrows flying into the air, and then they drew their swords and advanced. For a few moments there was much shrieking and the sound of apes falling to the ground. Very soon the apes realised they couldn't defeat such an impressive, highly trained force, so the ones still standing turned and fled into the bush. A group of injured, bleeding apes scattered the pathway.

The Princess approached one of the injured apes. 'Get up,' she commanded. Two of her women helped the ape to his feet. The ape eyed the Princess grudgingly. 'You are to come with us,' the Princess said.

They advanced to the top of the hill until they were outside the castle gates.

'I want you to tell them to open the castle gate,'
the Princess said to the ape.

For a moment the ape did nothing, but then seeming to realise the futility of not helping the Princess he let out a shrill whistle. The gates began to slide open.

They walked through the gates into the courtyard and there was another fierce but short battle as the Princess and her women defeated another group of apes. It wasn't long until the uninjured apes were fleeing through the castle gates into the tropical bush. Only Jed had the opportunity to use his sword when one ape got too close. He swung it wildly, but managed to slash the ape's arm and the creature retreated.

With the apes defeated the Princess led the way into the palace, shaking her head at the sight of the empty rooms and corridors. They walked through room after room without seeing any living thing.

'Where are the people?' said the Princess, more than once. 'Without people this castle has no life. It is a building with no soul. This place is like a graveyard!'

Then they came to one room and they were about to leave when the Princess noted movement from behind a large sofa. She indicated with a hand gesture to her women to move forward, which they did with stealth.

'Come out,' she commanded in a loud voice.

Slowly, rising to his feet, the children were bemused to see the braided hair of Chief Namba inching up. The little monkey, wearing a green waistcoat, was muttering to itself and pulling on the Chief's hair. Namba's eyes widened in horror when he saw he was surrounded by a dozen bare-shouldered women, the sights of their bows and arrows fixed on him.

'So Namba,' said the Princess finally. 'We meet again.'

Namba peered at her, his face creased into a frown.

'You don't remember me? I am Princess Makana, the ruler of Trinity Island. Ah, perhaps you don't recognise me, because last time you saw me you had caused me to become encased in a feeble, arthritic old body.'

'But – but–'

'Are you asking how I can be young again? That is because you didn't do your homework. If you had, you would know as soon as the Jewel Egg was restored by my own hand the curse would be broken.'

When Namba continued to stare at her, now with his mouth hanging open, the Princess became impatient. 'Stand up, you fool! Stop hiding behind that couch like a coward. Ladies, take this traitor to his cell.'

'Perhaps we should tie him up,' said Ethan. He rummaged in his backpack, and held out rope towards the Princess. 'He's very dangerous.'

'Good idea, Ethan,' said the Princess with approval. 'Ladies, tie him up and then take him to the dungeon.'

Two of Princess Makana's women helped Namba to his feet, expertly tied his hands behind his back and then began to push him from the room. To Kiri, the Chief seemed as though he had shrunk. With the loss of the Jewel Egg, he no longer had an aura of unrestrained, mad power. Instead he seemed broken and confused. The little monkey followed them, shrieking like he was laughing. Or was he crying? Kiri couldn't be sure. The Princess, the children and the rest of the women followed.

When they arrived at the dungeon, Kiri cleared her throat. 'Um, your Majesty. I have a key, if that would be helpful.'

'Yes, that would be most helpful,' said the Princess in a kind voice. Kiri handed over the large skeleton key, shyly.

The Princess's women locked Namba in the first cell and then systematically began opening the other cells. Inside were scores of sleeping parents, some of whom were wounded.

'What devilry is this?' said the Princess. 'Wake these people at once!'

The women walked through the cells and with the aid of smelling salts, people were soon stretching and getting to their feet. The Princess's women began helping the parents, tending to their injuries and bandaging their wounds.

The Princess's women opened the largest cell and there were Olaf and Daisy, flat on their backs, snoring loudly. Several women moved forward with the smelling salts, but for a moment they seemed to have no effect.

'Oh no,' said Ethan turning to Jed. 'I don't really want to hold their noses again.'

It was therefore a great relief when the giants suddenly snorted loudly and sat up – first Daisy and then Olaf.

'Oh, my darling!' said Daisy when she saw her husband. They embraced. The boys rolled their eyes, while Emma and Kiri smiled.

All around the children was the hustle and bustle of people moving around, and talking in muted whispers. The Princess stood at the end of the dungeon, resplendent in her gold dress and white coat. She raised her voice and majestically addressed the crowd. 'My fellow country people, the pretend Chief has been defeated and is now imprisoned.

The Jewel Egg is back in its rightful place. This is a historic day because Jewel Lagoon is now liberated!'

A huge cry of approval rose from the people while they cheered and applauded.

'Today I give you back liberty. Today I give you back your freedom. Today is the day when all wrongs will be righted. Step up, children from the Land of the Long White Cloud.' The children shuffled forward shyly and faced the group. 'Thanks to these children, today is the day we liberate *your* children!'

The crowd roared its approval and it was a moment before the Princess could speak again because of all the noise. 'Now my kin people – we are going to go and rescue your children! To the mines!'

The people began to stream out of the castle, following the Princess and her women.

'Oh, thank you, your Majesty,'
they said to the Princess if they were able to get near enough to her to say anything.

'Thank you, dear children,' they said to the children over and over, until the children didn't know what to say any more. The ground thundered with the footsteps of the two giants accompanying the group.

At the top of the mineshaft the crowd gathered, looking

anxious and fearful as the Princess's women disappeared under the earth.

'What about the apes?' some of them muttered. But it was soon apparent that the apes had fled and the Princess's women began to appear carrying the first of the rescued children on their backs.

'No resistance, ma'am,' said one of the women in a crisp voice to the Princess. There were sobs of joy as children were reunited with their parents, but as more and more children were brought to the surface, the Princess became angrier.

'How could he do this? These children have not only been locked up in a mine for five years, but they have been denied their right to see or to hear! Namba is despicable! What has he done with their eyes? What has he done with their ears?'

Kiri suddenly had a thought, and emptied her pockets. 'Your Majesty, do their eyes look like these before they get, um, attached?' she held up the pebbles. The people close by gasped. 'And their ears, do they look like these?' She held up the shells.

'Yes, my dear child. Where did you find them?' asked the Princess.

'They're in the palace, in this large room, all piled up.'

It was quickly decided that they would return to the castle, where Kiri led them to the room with the steel doors. The crowd of children and parents had been communicating with each other excitedly since being reunited, but when they saw the shells and pebbles, the room fell silent. Everyone gazed at Kiri while she stood by the precious piles.

'Kiri from the Land of the Long White Cloud, you know what to do,' said the Princess.

Kiri stared at her in confusion but then an idea came to her. She held the pebbles that had been in her pocket tightly in her closed hand and she could feel them warming.

'I think these below to someone.' She looked around the crowd. 'If you feel like they belong to you, please come forward.'

'If you have an itchiness and warmth under your eyelids, please come forward,' said the Princess. 'Don't be shy. Your eyes are waiting for you.'

At their words a little girl, who was very pretty under all the dirt, inched her way forward from midway through the crowd. She stood before Kiri and waited. Kiri wasn't sure what to do, but instinctively held the pebbles in front of the child's head. There was a flash of radiant light and for an instant Kiri had to close her eyes. When she opened them her hand was empty and the little girl was gazing at her with brilliant blue eyes.

'She can see,' cried a voice at the back of the room, and a murmur went through the crowd when the little girl ran and embraced her mother, easily picking her out from the crowd.

Kiri took the shells out from her pocket and held them up, motioning to the children to come forward. She spoke for the benefit of the parents. 'Please send your child forward. They may feel itchy where their ears should be.'

She had barely finished speaking when a young boy eagerly made his way towards her. He stood in front of her, his bright eyes full of expectation. Kiri held the shells, one in each hand, on either side of his head, there was another blinding flash and when she next looked her hands were empty and the little boy had pink, fleshy ears.

'Thank you,' he said in a clear voice, and once again there was a murmur from the crowd when he went back to his parents and they hugged him close.

Kiri turned to the Princess. 'I don't know–'

'It seems only right that children from the Land of the Long White Cloud have the power to restore to the innocent what has been denied them.' She gestured to the pile. 'Come Jed, Emma and Ethan, help Kiri restore sight and sound to the children of Trinity Island. Once you have restored these everything will go back to normal.'

'What's normal, your Majesty?'
asked Emma.

'On a child's second birthday they will receive the gift of sight and sound in a special ceremony with their parents. They will once again come to the palace and I or one of my representatives will do what you are now doing. But for now this is a task that I want only the four of you to do on this historic day.'

So it was that Kiri, Jed and the twins put their hands into

the pile of pebbles and shells and one by one the children came and stood before them to receive their missing eyes and ears. Afterwards it was like a dream. There was much celebrating and laughter. The Princess declared that the palace was open to everyone to use before they returned to their own homes. The children were whisked away by parents and returned sometime later freshly scrubbed and dressed in clean clothes. Without layers of soot and dirt the children looked quite different. They acted like different people, too. They laughed and played and chatted amongst themselves while a group of parents prepared a huge feast.

In the middle of all the festivities in the main hall, the four children snuck out and met each other in the corridor. Kiri consulted her now battered Elastic Island timetable.

'I don't know about you, but I'd like to get home soon,' she said to the others.

'I'm so pleased you've said that,' sighed Emma. 'I really miss home.'

The timetable was very complicated with many places the children had never heard of, and they were now looking at a different month from the month they had arrived, so the times were all altered. Between them they discovered the next Elastic Island service home was ten o'clock the next morning.

'Tomorrow we go home,' said Emma with a big smile, and all of them nodded happily at the thought.

Chapter 16

Time to Say Goodbye

A bustling, jostling, rather raucous group of people and creatures came to see the four children off. The Princess was there dressed in a flowing gold dress and a white and gold cape, with twenty of her women standing to attention in their white uniforms, this time without their bows and arrows and swords. There were also scores of parents and their children, all chattering excitedly. There were only minutes to go until Elastic Island was scheduled to arrive when there was a flutter of wings in the air.

'Big Wig!' cried Kiri. 'Wee Wig!'

The bow-tied, brightly coloured knockulouses landed gracefully on the ground in front of the children.

'We came to bid you safe travels,' said Big Wig, with a

little bow. 'It's been a pleasure to meet you and we do hope you will come and visit us again.'

'Oh, I'm going to miss you,' said Kiri.

'Me too!' said Emma.

'And me,' chirped Ethan.

'Ditto,' said Jed.

Big Wig looked a little embarrassed at their affectionate outburst, but then Wee Wig started chanting, 'Miss you! Miss you!' and they all laughed.

There was a sudden shout from the nearby river and the children turned towards the sound.

'Pangali!' cried Kiri, running towards the platypus, the other children following her.

'I just came to say farewell,' said Pangali. 'It's been so wonderful to meet you – you have changed my life. I will forever be in your debt!'

Pangali's family frolicked in the water behind him, looking at the four children curiously whenever they surfaced the water. His wife looked at them shyly. It was only after the children had promised they would visit the island again, and after much wet shaking of hands and webbed limbs (and a few tears), that they said their final goodbyes to the platypus and his family.

Then it was Olaf and Daisy's turn to say goodbye. Daisy was wearing a new flowery sundress and had bright purple lipstick on. She insisted on picking each of them up in turn to give them a kiss (something that Kiri imagined would give the boys nightmares for weeks afterwards).

'Are you sure I can't keep you?' Daisy asked Emma, when it was her turn.

'I really must go home,' said Emma firmly. 'Mum will be missing me.'

'I guess she will,' said Daisy, gently lowering her to the ground. 'A pretty little thing like you.'

Olaf shook their hands as gently as he could, although afterwards Kiri felt like her shoulder had been dislocated.

'I must be getting back to guarding the Jewel Egg,'
Olaf said, after they'd said their goodbyes.

'But darling, you promised me we'd have a holiday,' said Daisy. 'And don't forget the nice ladies who are now guarding the Jewel Egg. Look at them, so athletic and lovely in their little white uniforms. The Princess said you'd have help in the future.'

'I'd forgotten about them.' Olaf scratched his head. 'So, they don't need me there all the time to guard the Jewel Egg?'

'No, dear,' said Daisy patiently.

'Oh, that's all right then. So, my lovely wife, where do you want to go?'

Suddenly, the crowd around the children fell silent. Bugles sounded and the Princess stood in front of the children, her golden hair shining in the sunlight.

'Today my country people, we farewell the children of the Land of the Long White Cloud. Thanks to their courage we now can look forward to a new era of peace and prosperity in our lands. Thanks to them, evil has been defeated and good has been restored.

'Children, I ask you to give back your swords. You cannot take them to your country because they could easily fall into the wrong hands in your fair land, creating unnecessary danger for people around you. But rest assured they are here for you whenever you return to our lands if you desire them.'

Four of the Princess's women stepped forward and took the swords from each of the children with a small bow.

'However, children, I have a gift for each of you to take home,' continued the Princess. 'It is a small token of our thanks to you, and each of the gifts I trust you will find pleasing in different ways.'

The Princess nodded to another four of her women, and they each handed a wrapped gift to each child. The children ripped the wrapping open, Emma being the most careful with the paper.

Emma's gift was a necklace. It was a simple gold chain with a single jewel, pale blue in colour. Emma put it on and fingered the jewel, and felt immediately very peaceful and dreamy. She smiled. Ethan's gift was a new pair of spectacles. He whispered to Jed that it was a very odd gift because they didn't seem any different from his old pair. Nonetheless, he put his old spectacles in his backpack. Jed was clearly delighted with his gift. It was a watch that he soon discovered had all the different time zones for the countries that Elastic Island visited.

'Brilliant!' said Jed when he had opened his gift, and he promised the Princess they would definitely return.

Kiri was admiring her gift, which was a gold bracelet, when the Princess drew closer and whispered in her ear. 'Kiri, your gift will keep you and those close to you safe when danger is around you.'

Kiri examined the bracelet closely. It was gold and perfectly plain on the outside, but it had writing in a language she couldn't understand on the inside. It was a beautiful gift … although she couldn't see how a bracelet could keep anyone out of danger!

She was so busy looking at her bracelet that she didn't at first notice the noise coming from the bush. It was the sound of savagery and bloodlust. Placing the bracelet on her arm, she noted absently that the bracelet had changed shape. Instead of hanging loose around her wrist, it moulded to it instead. She looked up and was astonished to see Chief Namba storming the beach, jabbering at the top of his lungs like a man gone mad. Before anyone could move, he grabbed Emma and held her tightly to him with a knife at her throat. Emma looked like she was going to scream, but then Kiri saw her finger her new necklace and she returned Kiri's frantic gaze, looking cool and controlled.

'I'm going to kill her,' screamed the Chief. 'I'll kill all of you. I'm the ruler of this island. It is all mine! It's mine, I tell you.'

Several of the Princess's women tumbled from the bush, taking position to cover the Princess, their bows and arrows armed and ready.

'Sorry, ma'am,' panted one of them, her arm cut and bleeding. 'We were taking him some food, and we thought he was secure, but he'd managed to undo the bindings and he attacked us. I don't know where he got the knife from.'

'Injuries?'

'Two down, ma'am, but I think they'll pull through.'

'And he did this on his own?' the Princess muttered, clearly surprised

'I think that little monkey may have helped him. He was there with him, but he's now apprehended.'

'Were any apes with him?'

'No, ma'am. They've all run away.'

'Look at him,' muttered the Princess. 'He's acting like a lunatic.'

'Surrender!' Namba was shouting, froth dribbling from his mouth. His eyes bulged and his hand was shaking with anger. 'Surrender or I will kill this girl.'

'Shall I take him out?' muttered the woman with the cut arm, realigning her sights.

'Wait a moment,' said the Princess quietly as Kiri slowly stepped towards the madman and his captive.

'We're not surrendering to you,' shouted Kiri.

She began running at him, screaming at the top of her lungs. And then a remarkable thing happened. Kiri could see hundreds of Kiris running towards the crazed Chief and Emma out of the corner of her eye – and she could see herself and her other selves from multiple pairs of eyes, everything moving in slow motion. She saw Emma blink, and the Chief moved the knife a fraction of an inch closer to her neck. And then she suddenly had the knife in her own hand, and there was a deep gash on the Chief's arm, blood running down his thick biceps.

'On your knees, Namba.'

Kiri heard the Princess's command, but the words sounded like they came from a long way off. She felt rather than saw the Chief fall to his knees and at the same time, she dropped the knife and fell backwards on to the ground.

'Oh, Kiri,' she heard Emma cry.

Kiri closed her eyes and when she opened them again she was herself. She looked around her, blinking, and seeing things normally once more.

'How did you do that?' Jed said.

'What do you mean?'

'You turned into hundreds of you, and you were all charging at the Chief. And then, just like that,' said Jed, clicking his fingers, 'you had the knife out of his hand.'

'It must be something to do with the bracelet,' said Kiri slowly. She looked at the band and it was hanging loose on her wrist again.

'Look,' said Ethan. 'The Chief is shrinking!'

They turned to watch the Chief, who was kneeling in the sand. He *was* shrinking. They watched as his bones began shrivelling up and shortening, and as they did so he struggled to stand up in the sand. The Princess stepped forward and towered over him, her arms folded and her expression impassive. They continued to watch while his skin slowly dried and wrinkled, his braids shortened and his hair became white.

'What have you done to me?' cried Namba in an anguished voice. He stared at his wrinkled hands, turning them over and over.

'I've done nothing to you,' said the Princess. 'You've done this to yourself. If you had done your research properly you would never have cursed me in the first place.'

'What do you mean?'

'You would have known it was too dangerous. Whoever curses another person and encases them in an old body runs the risk of having the same thing happen to them also.'

'But how?'

'You tried to kill a child that was with me when the Jewel Egg was restored. But it was not her blood that was spilt, but your own, so now you suffer the consequences.'

Namba let out a feeble cry of anguish. 'Change me back,' he croaked, in a broken voice.

'I can't,' said the Princess. 'This time the curse is irreversible. Ladies, take him to the cells!'

'What will happen to him now?' asked Ethan, watching Namba being taken away. He hobbled feebly on his feet, muttering and wailing to himself. He was only recognisable by the jewel and bone necklace that he wore.

'In the future, I will let him go,' said the Princess.

'But how can you do that?' Ethan sounded incensed. 'He killed your mother! He imprisoned the children in the mines. He is a monster!'

'Yes, he was a monster. But this land is done with vengeance and death. He can do me no harm now that he is in a weakened old body. He will have to live whatever years he has left with the knowledge of all the wickedness he has inflicted here. He will die, one day, alone and unloved. That is punishment enough. I won't let him go straight away, however; for the time being he will be safer locked up. The apes aren't known for their loyalty, and as for the people – well, best if he is out of harm's way until things settle down again. But one day in the future, I will let him go.'

The Princess looked up to the horizon and then returned her beautiful gaze to the four children. 'Now dear children, your ride home is here. It is time for us to say goodbye until we see you again. Good luck and bon voyage!'

When the Princess finished speaking the crowd began to clap and there was a whooshing sound as Elastic Island hugged the bay they were gathered in.

'All aboard,' cried Mr Jollybowler, waving his bowler hat at the children. 'Ah, it's the four children from Browns Bay. Welcome back! It's nice to have you travelling with us again today. I must confess I was very concerned when I didn't see you on the return journey we had originally talked about. I really wondered what had happened to you, but then I thought, what could go wrong on a beautiful tropical island like this? The only thing to worry about is remembering not to sit under a coconut tree. If you do, you might have a coconut fall on your head. I've heard that falling coconuts can give you a real headache.'

The children exchanged glances.

'Um, Mr Jollybowler, do you know anything about the islands you visit?' asked Emma. 'I mean, do you stop off and visit them yourself?'

'Goodness, no!' exclaimed Mr Jollybowler. 'I don't have land legs, you see. Being on land makes me sick. And really, I'm much too busy piloting Elastic Island to dawdle about taking sightseeing trips. That's for the likes of you and my other customers, not me.'

'So some of the islands you visit could be dangerous and you wouldn't know?' asked Emma.

'Dangerous? Certainly not! Part of Rinaldo the parrot's job is to read all the travel guides so we can inform passengers of everything they need to know about their chosen destination. It's all part of our luxury service.'

'But Rinaldo's a parrot. Can he read?' asked Ethan. 'And if he can read, does he understand English? After all, he's an Italian parrot, isn't he?'

'Goodness, I never thought to ask him if he could read, or what language he could read in. Rinaldo, you can read, and read in English, can't you?'

Rinaldo looked at him in disgust.
'Are you questioning my honour?' he screamed.

'Of course not, of course not,' Mr Jollybowler said hastily, and he whispered to the children. 'I'll ask him again after he's had lunch. He's always grumpy before lunch. Now I take it we are journeying back home to Browns Bay? You don't want to visit Candy Island or Banana Split Bay today by any chance?'

'Browns Bay, please,' said Emma, before anyone else could say a word.

'Give us your biglietto! Your biglietto,' cried Rinaldo the parrot.

Just when the children thought they would have to be singing to pay their fare home, the crowd on the shore broke into song. The children didn't recognise the music, but they could hear the voices of some of the friends they had made in their adventures as part of the harmony. Pangali's small voice rose up clear and true, Olaf's voice deep and out of tune, the knockulouses chirpy and bright.

'Hold on! No time for pre-ride drinks this time, we're running a little behind schedule,' cried Mr Jollybowler as the sand began stretching out to sea. 'Here we gooooooo …'

Elastic Island snapped them out far into the ocean, and each of them hugged a tree closely, the wind whistling past their faces. It seemed only a minute and then they were standing opposite the cliffs at Browns Bay.

'Home,' mouthed Emma, tears filling her eyes.

'Good day, dear children,' said Mr Jollybowler as they disembarked. 'It's been a pleasure to have you travelling with Elastic Island. We appreciate you have a choice of different transport alternatives and look forward to seeing you again in the future.'

'Yes, definitely,' said Jed, checking his new watch as he stood on the sand at the edge of Browns Bay Beach. 'Curious,' he muttered to himself. 'We seem to have arrived on the same day we left, but half an hour before the time we left.'

'Oops,' said Mr Jollybowler. 'Sometimes we get a bit of time distortion. Mind you, half an hour shouldn't be a problem, should it children? I remember once we were out by one thousand years – now that was a nuisance!'

'Problema! Problema!' squawked Rinaldo the parrot, and before anyone else had the chance to say anything Elastic Island had disappeared.

The children stood on the familiar beach of home and Kiri let out a long sigh. 'That was an amazing adventure, but it's good to be home.'

'It almost seems like a dream now,' said Emma.

'Oh, you don't have your dream book anymore!' said Kiri. 'It's back on Trinity Island.'

'We can get it next time we go back.' Emma clutched her pendant. 'But then again, maybe I don't need it anymore. Maybe it doesn't matter what our dreams mean. Maybe it just matters what we do when we are awake.'

The four of them walked down the beach to where the girls' discarded towels still lay. Kiri flopped herself down and gazed out to sea. Jed continued to examine his watch, muttering under his breath about the different time zones in places they had never heard of. Emma gazed towards the sleeping forms of her parents and then went and sat by them.

'Hello dear,' said her mother, waking up when Emma approached. 'Have you had a nice afternoon?'

'It's been very … very … um … pleasant,' Emma finally responded. 'Yes, very pleasant, all in all.' Kiri looked over as Emma touched her pendant. She looked very content.

'Your dress looks different,' said her mother. 'It seems

more sparkly … and I'm sure it's longer than first thing this morning.'

'Really?' said Emma in a calm voice. 'But that would be impossible.'

'Yes, I suppose you're right,' said her mother, lying back. 'Perhaps I've had enough sun for one day. We probably should go home soon.'

Down on the beach Ethan was rummaging in his backpack. 'Anyone for a peanut butter sandwich?' he asked no one in particular.

'No!' said Kiri. 'You've got to be joking. Are you trying to give us food poisoning? Eat it yourself.'

'No thanks, mate,' said Jed.

'Oh, this is weird,' said Ethan after a moment.

'You mean you're weird, knucklehead,' said Kiri. She was studying her bracelet. It had moulded to her wrist again.

'No, I mean my glasses. I can suddenly see directly behind me. Those three guys from school that like to pick on me are walking towards us. Oh great! I'd forgotten about them.'

Kiri rose to her feet and Jed turned to stare past Ethan's back. 'Crikey, you're right,' said Jed. 'Those morons are coming to have another go at you. I think this time they're going to get a surprise.'

Kiri and Jed exchanged looks. 'Are you thinking what I'm thinking?' she said.

'What are we going to do?' said Ethan.

'Well, I think attack is the best form of defence,' said Jed mildly. 'How about we chase them this time? Follow me!'

Jed let out a loud roar and started running towards the trio of thugs; Kiri started screaming loudly and joined in the chase. Ethan followed, yelling at the top of his voice, 'We're coming to get you!'

To this day, the fat boy, the boy with the shaved head and the child with the large nose don't go to Browns Bay Beach. Kiri heard through some friends of friends that they say the last time they went there three wild apes suddenly charged down the beach screeching at them. For Kiri, Jed and Ethan it was a funny sight. They had only just started running towards the trio when the thugs turned and fled.

'Gosh, I didn't expect it to be that easy,' said Ethan happily.

Kiri watched while her bracelet returned to normal, hanging loose on her wrist. 'Well don't get too confident – it might not happen again.'

Jed disappeared for a while and returned with ice creams for them all. 'Gee, thanks,' said Ethan.

'That's nice of you,' said Kiri. 'Thanks.'

Emma waved at them from under her parents' orange sun umbrella, also eating ice cream.

'So …' said Jed, scratching the sand absentmindedly with his foot. 'Being school holidays and all – where do you want to go tomorrow?'

With Thanks

Many thanks to publisher Chrissy Metge and her enthusiasm for *Elastic Island Adventures*. A big thank you to a talented trio — Dmitry Chizhov for the illustrations, Craig Violich for the book design, and India Lopez for editing the book. Thanks to my wonderful agent, Susanne Theune. Thank you to my husband, Iain, for allowing me to revert back to being a ten-year-old while writing this adventure. A special thank you to Milla McKenzie-Brown for adding to the fun of the experience of writing this book. Milla is currently helping me research and develop ideas for book two of the *Elastic Island Adventures* series, so keep an eye out for the second book in the future!

About the Author

Karen McMillan has written a bunch of bestselling books for adults, but *Elastic Island Adventures* is her first book for children.

Find out more about Karen at www.karenm.co.nz